I0544077

A THRILLER

THE WISDOM OF
SOLOMON

CRUEL MESSENGER BOOK 1

TIMOTHY W. AYERS

This is a work of fiction. Names, characters, places, and incidents are products of the author's imagination or are used fictitiously and are not to be construed as real. Any resemblance to actual events, locations, organizations, or persons, living or dead, is entirely coincidental.

World Castle Publishing, LLC
Pensacola, Florida
Copyright © Timothy W. Ayers 2019
Paperback ISBN: 9781950890408
eBook ISBN: 9781950890415
First Edition World Castle Publishing, LLC, July 29, 2019
http://www.worldcastlepublishing.com

Licensing Notes
All rights reserved. No part of this book may be used or reproduced in any manner whatsoever without written permission, except in the case of brief quotations embodied in articles and reviews.
Cover: Karen Fuller

DEDICATION

There are two women that I dedicate this book to. One is my mother Edna, who the mother character was named after. To be quite honest there is more fact than fiction in the Edna line of the story.

The other is Marylee. I started the book right after heart surgery, and she has listened and commented on every word of it since the day I began. Thanks, Marylee. And Mom, I miss you.

PROLOGUE

Mahmood rose early from his thin floor mattress and breathed out a cloud of warm, moist air into the cold Afghanistan morning. He knew the work ahead of him and had made peace with himself over it. Yet doubts, guilt, and sadness consumed his soul.

On this beautiful day, under the bright blue sky of his homeland, he had purged his soul of his sinful thoughts. Soon he would step through the gates of paradise. Instead of intensely desiring a single slender, pretty infidel virgin, he would be in paradise with seventy-two who shared his faith.

So his faith promised, but his heart screamed in anger.

Mahmood removed a package from its hiding place, the first time he had touched it since the day he picked it up from a messenger of Sabawoon Habibi, leader of the local Taliban. He unrolled the chador from around the thick package and re-rolled it around the note he'd struggled to write last night.

He unwrapped the front page of a local newspaper underneath the cloth, the last barrier between him and the explosives that would bring his death. He had not touched the vest since the day he had picked it up.

As he strapped the explosive vest across his chest and placed his perahan tunban tunic over it, his mind went over and over his instructions regarding the group of college-aged American missionaries from Co-Exist, for which he had worked as translator and guide these last three months. He pushed his way through Jalalabad on that brisk morning and finally arrived at the compound for the Americans. The Taliban guards who had kept the Americans alive and safe, as agreed by Sabawocn Habibi to Rev. Amin, ignored him, as usual. As with previous groups, no one had questioned how Rev. Amin was able to forge a deal with the Taliban to provide for the safety of the Co-Exist groups, even though war and guns filled his country. Instead, the foolish American politicians, leaders, and pastors who supported his ministry thanked him for the protection that allowed them to work freely in the countryside around Jalalabad, constructing homes, digging wells, and teaching the male children.

Mahmood entered the gates of the American compound, and the twenty missionaries due to leave later that afternoon rushed into the courtyard to welcome him one last time. He had befriended each...even Gloria Beck. When she neared, his skin tingled, his words became stiff, and her presence clouded his mind.

To them, he was their friend who had taught them Afghan culture and tutored them in the Pashto language. In their eyes, he had helped them accomplish their mission to show both Christians and Muslims how they could work together to meet the needs of the poor and weak.

As required by the Taliban, Gloria and all of the young females wore a chador wrapped around their heads, and their clothing appropriately covered their skin. But their adherence to each of the restrictions meant nothing. Today they would discover why Rev. Amin was able to forge a deal with the terrorists, what his end of the bargain entailed.

He knew what he had to do, but his overwhelming desire to protect Gloria from it had driven him to adjust the instructions given to him.

He dared to brush a hand against the fabric wrapped around

her head. "Gloria, I noticed your chador was fraying, and I picked up another for you at the market in town." He handed her the gift.

She smiled under her veil. He couldn't see it on her mouth, but her eyes expressed it.

"I thank you deeply. I will treasure this, and my time here, the rest of my life," she responded in Pashto.

"I must also return to you your phone. It must have fallen out of your pocket while we worked yesterday. I picked it up, but I forgot it was in my tunic when we returned." His smile dimmed at the thought of the video he had recorded on the phone to explain his actions to her, but she seemed not to notice.

"Oh, thank you! I looked all over for it last night. Now I will be able to watch movies during the long flight." She laughed, and it sounded like music to Mahmood, a music forbidden on many levels, but it momentarily made him happy.

"Go and place the chador in your room and join us again before our last meal together."

Gloria trotted the one hundred yards to her dwelling. As the door closed behind Gloria, Mahmood, believing she would be safe, ripped open his tunic and cried the prayer, "Allahu Akbar!"

* * *

Right before the door clicked behind her, Gloria thought she heard Mahmood call out to her. She opened the door halfway when a bright light exploded outside.

Fire ate the air. An intense shock wave pounded against the door. It knocked her back inside with such intensity that she hit the floor, the last thing she remembered before blacking out.

When she roused, she peered out the door at the smoking devastation. Dead, her friends were all dead. Except her.

One thought filled her. Her dear, sweet Mahmood had been a terrorist—someone who viewed her people only as infidels who deserved death. Someone who hated her people enough to kill himself in order to accomplish it.

They thought he'd been like them, wanting to help the people of the world. Instead, he left this earth and took them with him. She pulled her knees up to her chest and bawled. How deceived she and her friends had been!

CHAPTER 1

Three months later

"Your dad stopped by with Orval Miller last night," Mom said as I plopped down in a chair next to her bed at the Baptist Senior Home in the North Hills of Pittsburgh.

If her mind was drifting through memories from other times and other places, this would be a long morning. In spite of the fact that Dad had been dead for three years, I held my tongue. In my daily visits over the last year, I'd learned not to try bringing her back from jaunts into her alternate universe. In time I learned, like many loved ones of Alzheimer's patients, that it was better to sit, listen, and love. More difficult, but better for everyone.

At least this time she hadn't drifted all the way off. Dad's old friend, Orval, was elderly, but still very much alive. "It's always good to see Orval." I allowed my own mind to wallow in the past for a moment. Mom's stroke had been the last in a series of bad events that started with my father's cruel battle with cancer. It beat him, at least what was left of the bigger-than-life person everyone but my family called the Reverend Doctor Joshua Cameron. Then the strain of his death left Mom with a stroke, followed rapidly by oncoming Alzheimer's.

My devotion to Mom was a little greater than my younger brother's. Zach kept Mom's finances straight and paid out the medical bills. My job was to sit and listen to Mom's stories. And, oh, did she have some great stories to tell.

"So how did the visit with Dad and Mr. Miller go?" I asked.

"Your dad looks better than ever. Heaven must really agree with him. He's put back on all the weight he lost when he was sick. Best of all, he says they let him preach as long as he wants." She gave a quick clap and her eyes flashed with a momentary twinkle of joy.

"That should make Dad happy. He never was much for watching the clock when it came to preaching." It wasn't the first time she said Dad had visited. He rarely came with a friend though, especially a living friend. "What did Mr. Miller have to say?" I asked.

"Well, Zach—"

"I'm Jude, Mom. I'm the oldest of your two boys. Zach is the younger brother with the bald head. I'm the older one, who's a detective." I needed to keep that straight. She already thought most of my gifts to her were from some guy in Germany named George. Interesting, since none of us knew of any history of a gentleman named George in her real life.

"Well, sometimes I get a little confused, and since you don't visit much it's hard to remember you sometimes," Mom said playfully, with her well remembered crooked smile.

"Mom, I'm here every day."

It was nice to see a hint of the woman that used to play games with my brother and me in the back pew of church during the long Sunday evening services. Like I said, Dad never was one for clock-watching once he took the pulpit.

"What did Mr. Miller have to say?" I asked again.

"How did you know he was here?" Mom said it as if she was genuinely surprised that I knew of the visit. She was drifting again but quickly got back on track. "But it is funny that you should ask, because Deacon Miller wanted to talk to you. I told him you weren't here, and that seemed to bother him." She stopped in mid-thought to point to her bed stand. "Could you hand me the Ensure, dear?"

Mom took a sip. "You know, they are so good to me here at the school."

I shook my head. Her shifts between her alternate realities were giving me whiplash. So, now we were in the days when she had been the president of the school board. It probably made her time at the home more pleasant to think she was back in a period when she was vital to both her family and her community.

She took another sip. "Whenever I want one of these drinks, I just knock on the door to the restaurant and yell—"

I finished the story with her and we both said together "— Yoo-hoo!" This was probably the hundredth time I'd heard the tale.

Mom giggled at our little joke. I prodded her back on topic. "What did Mr. Miller say?"

"Like I was saying before you interrupted me, he wanted to talk to you. Once he saw you weren't here, he was a little distressed. So I offered to give you a message. He said, 'two-fifteen,' then he grabbed your dad's arm and off they went down the hall." Story finished, she laid back on her bed.

I spread my arms in front of me. "I have no idea what he could mean by that. You know what, Mom, I'll swing by his office today and ask him." If I left soon, I would still have time to visit him before my shift started at noon.

Mom's eyes started to close. "Yes, do that. He seemed so upset." She paused, and her eyes closed completely. A moment later, they snapped open. "And please tell him thank you for visiting your dad." Mom closed her eyes again, and a peaceful look crossed her face.

It was nap time, and that was my cue to go.

CHAPTER 2

I had just slid behind the wheel of my vintage Chevelle SS 396 when my two-way chirped on my cell phone. "Detective Cameron," I answered.

"Jude, this is Ed. Some kids just found a body in the alley behind the projects on the north side. I'm heading there now. How close are you?"

"Be there in ten minutes." After playing guess-the-memory-zone game with Mom, I didn't even complain about being called in early. I picked up Interstate 279 and shot straight to the projects. I parked just beyond the yellow tape marking off the crime scene and found Ed leaning against one of the black and whites, scrolling through pictures on the photographer's SLR. He handed me a set of photos.

Cheryl McKinnis, the city's coroner, snapped off her rubber gloves while barking orders at the cops nearby. That was the way Cheryl handled all her situations: work hard, play hard — and her joy at being in control sparkled in her eyes. She waved me and Ed over to the gurney where the body lay.

You'd think the next part would get easier with each lifeless body. Not so. I always thought about whose mother, father, brother, sister, son or daughter it was on the gurney before me. It would never get easier.

"No ID on him," Cheryl explained. "As far as we can see, the old guy must have wandered into the wrong place and paid the price. Looks like robbery and murder, but that's just a quick opinion. I won't have much more until after the autopsy."

As Cheryl pulled open the body bag, I sucked in a breath hard and loud.

Ed looked right at me and asked, "You know him?"

"Yeah," I choked out. "Orval Miller. He was an old friend of my folks…and my Sunday school teacher when I was kid." I shook my head and looked away. "Who would have done this? Orval was a good man. I considered him a mentor." My anger toward God flared again. First He took Dad, letting him suffer like he did, then He took away Mother's mind. Now He had allowed Orval to bleed out on the cold, dirty concrete. It was too much. I could feel the heat creep up my neck to my face as my jaw tightened. Orval's dead body was one more sour element in my relationship with God.

The world around me went quiet. All I heard was melting snow as it dripped off the rooftops and splashed into the dirty puddles below, reverberating like gunfire in my ears.

I turned to face Ed. "This is strange. I was just talking to my mother about Mr. Miller. She said he came to visit her last night."

"That makes your mom a suspect." Ed was a good cop, but he'd been around for a long time. Like all cops close to retirement, he had seen enough to make him cynical. This time, his dry humor failed to bring even a smile.

"She said he came with my dad."

"He'd be a suspect too, if I hadn't gone to his funeral three years ago." Ed added another attempt at lightening my mood.

I snapped out my fog and asked Cheryl, "What happened?"

"It was bullet shot to the heart. Scuff marks indicate a struggle, at least as much as the old man could muster. He was robbed, since his wallet was missing, so that could have been the motive. I place the time of death around 2:30 a.m."

A uniformed officer approached. "Do you want us to start

knocking on doors to find out if anyone saw anything?"

"Yeah, go ahead," Ed responded. "Call me if you get any leads." Then he turned to me. "So what did your Mother say about Mr. Miller's visit?"

"That was pretty strange, too. She said he actually came to talk to me and that he seemed distressed when I wasn't there. Before he left, he gave her a message for me. He said, 'two-fifteen.' What that means, I don't know."

Ed rubbed his jaw — a movement he made when preparing to give me some advice. "Your mom was a pretty amazing lady before your dad died. But Jude, you've got to admit, she's not on this earth most of the time. Some cryptic message from a dead man to an Alzheimer patient is not exactly hard and fast evidence. If you ask me, it was a gang banger. Lots of them live here." Ed gestured with both palms up at the crumbling buildings that housed many of the city's poor.

Somehow the gang banger scenario didn't fit what I knew about the old man. "You didn't know Deacon Miller. He had a burden, as he called it, for the kids in gangs who lived near the church. He paid for basketball courts, after-school tutors, activities for children, and he sponsored every event the projects put on." I ticked his good deeds off on my fingers. "Most of the kids knew him. He was one of the few men who could walk safely through these dangerous streets at night."

"But it would only take one. If he was strung out on crack, he might have seen him as an easy mark."

"You might be right, but you're the one who taught me to assume nothing." I stared down at Orval's cold, lifeless body. It was hard not to think of his animated movements as he taught our junior high Sunday school class. He taught Bible stories like he had walked the dusty roads with the Apostles themselves. When I was a kid, we often joked that he was old enough to have actually done that. Now, I looked at him and realized that he was

13

a man taken long before his time.

Cheryl poked my arm. "Since you seem to know the victim, can you tell me if he had any close relatives in the area?"

"Yeah, a daughter, Izzie — excuse me, Councilwoman Isabella Miller," I corrected.

"Izzie, huh? You've got history with that chick. Serious history, as I remember?" Ed reminded me.

"Yep, we started in the church nursery — Mom called it the cradle roll — and we went through every grade together." The memories brought my first smile since I arrived on the scene.

Ed rolled his eyes. "Jude, you know what I mean. Romantic history."

"I guess you could say that. She said I loved my job more than her. She bailed before we got serious." I zipped up the body bag. I couldn't take looking at Orval this way any more.

"Before you got serious? Jude, you had to return the engagement ring. Man, you're rewriting history," Ed scoffed.

"Cheryl," I said as I swiveled toward Cheryl. "I know how hard Izzie is going to take this. Let me be the one to tell her. I owe her that much. She just lost her mom a year ago. She and her dad were close."

"I think we can let you do the honors. Just remember, this is an open case: don't give away any information." She motioned for two of the officers. "You can take it to the morgue now."

"How quick can we get the autopsy done?" I asked.

"Amazingly, my dear, it's been a good week in Pittsburgh, so I'll actually start on this right away." Cheryl knew I was hurting; if she were a touchy-feely type she might have given me a hug.

I walked to my car and called back over my shoulder, "I'll meet you at the station, Ed. I also ask that you don't rush to judgment on this one. The gang banger theory just doesn't wash for me. My police gut says there is a lot more to this one than what we see."

CHAPTER 3

The drive to Izzie's apartment on Forbes Avenue didn't take long, but once there, I hesitated. I fingered the key to her apartment on my key ring. Though tempted to use it to let myself in, I thought better of it.

The reverberating sound of my knock in the hallway had a familiar ring that brought back warmer times. A familiar sound that I missed.

"Hey, Jude." She almost sang the words as she opened the door. Her dark, untamed curls fell across her forehead and curved around each cheek, caressing the small dimples that deepened with the intensity of her wide, toothy smile. I didn't want to look into her eyes. Those immense flickering pools always drew out of me things I didn't want to reveal or tell or even admit to myself.

As much as it thrilled me to hear her say my name and stare again at her beautiful face, I didn't smile. I wasn't here to talk over old times.

"I wish I could say I was here for a personal call, but I'm afraid I'm here on official business."

Her hand went to her mouth. She knew police business almost always brought bad news. "Oh no, Jude. It's not your mother, is it?"

I shook my head. "No, Iz." I took her soft, small hands in mine, walked her to the couch in front of her living room window, and sat down next to her. "It's about your dad. They found him dead

15

in an alley in the projects this morning—" My throat tightened, and I could say no more.

"Wha—what do you mean? He's in the projects all the time."

"We're not sure what happened. It could have been a robbery or a gang banger..."

"No, no. That wouldn't happen." She shook her head and her curls bounced, catching the sunlight streaming through the window. "I don't believe that for one minute," she stated adamantly before breaking into deep, heavy sobs.

I pulled her toward me and wrapped my arms around her. "I'm sorry, Izzie. I'm so sorry."

I remembered what a perfect fit her petite and toned body had been for my arms, how comfortable it was for her head to rest against my shoulder. We sat that way until her soft sobbing quieted.

Isabella snatched some tissues off the coffee table, blew her nose, and dried her eyes. "I just can't believe it, Jude. You know everything Dad has done for the kids down there. They love him. He was like everybody's granddad."

"I know, Iz. Can you think of anyone else that would want to kill him?" I slipped from old lover back to detective too easily. She had been right about my misplaced love. Every argument we had was about my job. I saw it as a calling, and she saw it as my escape from committing my heart to her completely.

"I knew something was wrong when Dad didn't call and say goodnight. I talked to him earlier in the day, and he seemed very distracted, almost disturbed. When I pushed him about his tone he promised he would tell it all to me today when we had dinner."

"Do you know what his schedule was yesterday? Did he have plans to meet someone last night?"

Izzy flashed that look she often gave me in the past when I turned on the cop side of me. But for her own protection, I needed

16

some answers.

"We only talked for a second, yesterday, and that was to set up dinner for tonight. I was in council meetings all yesterday evening and then went out for dinner and drinks with the mayor and a few others. Cal, a friend from the mayor's office, dropped me off about two a.m." I jotted that note down mentally.

She stood and wrapped her arms around herself. "I need to be alone, Jude. Thank you for being the one to tell me. You know Dad always thought the world of you." With that she opened the door.

For an awkward moment, I just stared at the door. There was nothing else I could do or say to ease her pain, so I left. But the old feelings came with me. I would never get used to not being with her.

CHAPTER 4

By the time I arrived at the station, Ed was waiting for me in the circa 1950 chair behind my slightly newer desk. The chair creaked when he stood and handed me the papers he'd been reading.

I glanced at them—the CSI preliminary report and some leads shaken out by officers combing the area. Ed told me what he knew so far.

"Two of the neighbors saw Orval Miller with one of the street kids. He is a known gang member and doesn't have a great reputation. He also has several priors. I think we have enough to make him a 'person of interest.'" Ed said the last phrase with derision. Nothing about Ed Rivers was PC, and he let you know it.

"Uniforms found a gun in one of the garbage bins. It was recently shot. They're checking it for prints now. I'm hoping ballistics can do a rush on it."

"Who's the suspect?"

"His street name is LoDee. The name his mother gave him is Lorenzo Deets. I think we should pay him a little visit," Ed said with a smile. "Let's think positive on this one. We'll bring him back here, get the confession, and head over to Tom's for a burger and beer to celebrate."

"Something doesn't add up." I couldn't explain the uneasiness inside me.

"Take it from an old timer, Cameron." Ed backhanded my arm. "These kids aren't that smart. That's why our juvie hall is full. Most of them go on to be career criminals and fill our cells as well. Get used to it, kid." Ed headed over to the coffee maker to grab a cup of our less-than-robust joe. "By the way, how did Councilwoman Miller take the news?"

"As best as can be expected when you find out your father was murdered." I paused and thought about what I was going to say. "She doubted it was gang related. She said most kids looked up to him, like he was their granddad. There may be something to that. My gut tells me we need to dig a little deeper."

Ed dismissed Izzie's comments with a wave of his hand. "The captain wants this one tied up fast. Miller was a high-profile citizen, and the papers are all over him to catch the killer. Even the Mayor's office is climbing up his back on this one."

Maybe Ed was right. Maybe this was just as simple as it seemed to be. Often the simplest answer was the right one. But the whole thing still settled about as well as vinegar and baking soda. I wanted to look at all the angles, but Ed Rivers had already made up his mind.

"Did she know if her dad was meeting with someone last night?" he asked as he filled a cup with a sludge of coffee.

I filled him in then added, "We should call his secretary at his office."

"All done, partner, but she said some full-of-himself, kid attorney of the Mayor's already went through Miller's office. No hurry to search it now. Thought we could swing by later on today. Let's go catch us a killer." Ed pulled me to my feet. I didn't have time to question what the Mayor's office was doing interfering with our investigation, before we were out the door.

As I drove back to the projects Ed pulled out two copies of Lorenzo Deets's mugshot. "This is what the kid looks like. We can try Mugger's Park first, to see if he hangs out there." Mugger's

Park was Ed's nickname for the rundown city park the gangs used for meetings.

We drove the blocks around the area before pulling up to Mugger's Park. Ed's instinct was right. LoDee leaned against a chain link fence when we pulled up.

Rivers took the lead. "Lorenzo Deets?" At the kid's nod, he introduced us both. "Do you have a minute? We have a few questions for you."

Deets shrugged.

"Listen, LoDee — or do you prefer Lorenzo?" Ed kept his tone warm and friendly.

"Whatever," LoDee said, his head hanging down. "It don't make no difference. I know why you're here. You're lookin' for one of the street kids to take the fall for Deacon Miller. So it don't matter what I say." He answered in a way that made me think he had been standing there waiting for the cops to come.

I exchanged a glance with my partner. Word had a way of spreading.

Ed straightened and took a deep breath. "We understand you were with Orval Miller last night. Can you give me any details on your conversation?"

Before the kid could answer, Ed's phone rang. "Detective Rivers." He placed his hand over part of the phone and whispered, "It's forensics." He listened for a moment. "Yeah, who?" He glanced at LoDee. Then he pocketed his phone with a 'spider to the fly' grin spreading across his face and pulled cuffs out.

"Lorenzo Deets, you're under arrest for the murder of Orval Miller. The lab just told me they found your prints on the murder weapon. How do you explain that?"

The kid rolled his eyes, then gave him an I-told-you-so look. I looked at the kid's. It was like he expected that to happen as well. My stomach flipped. My gut was screaming at me, but the evidence was talking louder.

Ed didn't wait for any more of an answer before he spun the kid around and snapped handcuffs on him, then recited his Miranda Rights. I gazed on in surprise. Once again everything seemed too easy — too arranged.

LoDee didn't say a word on the way to the station. He was quiet up until we walked into the interrogation room and laid the weapon on the table. "Is this your gun?"

Genuine shock crossed LoDee's face. "Used to be."

"What do you mean?"

"Deacon Miller did a gun exchange last week. He bought a lot of guns from us for fifty bucks each. I needed money to buy my mom a birthday gift, so I turned it in," he told us.

Ed pushed himself away from the table, threw his hands into the air, spun around a full circle, leaned in four inches from Deets's face and mocked, "That has got to be the worst story I have ever heard." Ed slammed his palms on the table. "'Oh, Officer, it used to be my gun, but I sold it to the man who was killed with it.' Real believable, LoDown. Excuse me, I mean LoDee." It was a lot of show, but when you play the bad cop, you have to play it big.

"So you're saying you sold it to Mr. Miller at his exchange?" I clarified with my good-cop tone.

"Yeah, I started meetin' up with Deacon Miller for some Bible study then started goin' to the First Baptist youth group—"

"Kid, the youth pastor at First Baptist is friend of mine. I can call him right now to see if you're lying. So think about what you're saying."

"Go ahead and call. Pastor Charlie will tell the truth. He knew I was in that Bible study thing." The boy looked me in the eyes, then let out a long sigh and slumped down in his chair. "I guess I better ask for a lawyer."

"I've heard enough of this bull, Jude. The interview is over. I'm taking the kid down to booking." Ed grabbed LoDee by the arm and dragged him out of his chair and through the door. I sucked in a breath, shook my head and walked slowly back to my desk.

The interrogation raised the uneasiness in my gut to a new level. I was starting to hear Dad's words from many of his sermons. "If we only had the wisdom of Solomon, then we could figure out the world's problems." That was what I wished for. There was a time when I would have prayed for it, but I hadn't been a praying man for three years. This time, though, I whispered a soft and short prayer, "Lord, give me the wisdom of Solomon."

I swore I heard my dad's chuckle, clear enough that I spun around to see who else was in the hallway.

No one was there.

CHAPTER 5

LoDee's story was easy enough to check out. While Ed booked Deets and filled out the papers, I headed to Dad's old church to see my childhood friend Charlie Hall. We'd played every known sport with each other. We hadn't quite been inseparable, but it had been hard to find a day when we were apart.

I walked in the church's back door. It just didn't feel right to go in the front like I was a regular attender.

At my knock on his office door, Charlie called out without looking up from whatever he was writing. "Come in. Can I help you?"

"Yeah, someone told me this church had a half-baked youth pastor, and I wanted to check him out." I had a wall between me and God, and ever since Charlie returned from seminary and Dad hired him as the youth pastor, he had been on the other side of it. But that couldn't keep me from giving him a hard time like I used to do.

Charlie never looked up, but his eyes crinkled at the corners. "Well, if you lie down with dogs, you come up with fleas. I guess I've been running with the wrong pack." He dropped his pen and jumped up.

"Jude, it's so good to see you." He came around the desk with a big smile and pumped my hand up and down with a tight grip.

His smile faded quickly as he perched on the edge of his

desk. "You don't have to tell me about Mr. Miller. The story has already circulated. Everyone knows, but no one can believe it. Any suspects?"

"You know there is, Charlie," I said as I slipped into a chair. "What can you tell me about Lorenzo Deets?"

"Hey, quit being a cop for a second." The wall between us seemed to expand and fill the room.

"I will as soon as this case is over. Can you help me?"

"If you coach one of my basketball teams," he tossed back at me.

"I'm not ready yet. Give me a few months or years or decades."

"Thought I'd try. What do you want to know about LoDee?"

"Everything."

"Deacon Miller led him to Christ about a month ago and was having a regular Bible study with him. LoDee joined the youth group and was showing the signs of fruit that we all look for. I was encouraged." Charlie's face scrunched up in confusion. I knew there was more.

"And what else?"

"Deacon Miller stopped in two days ago. He was going to his Sunday school classrooms to prepare for the upcoming lesson. Usually I can count on him to lift me up, give me good counsel and then pray with me. Instead, he seemed nervous and jumpy. He only stayed long enough to say hello. I'd never seen him like that before."

"We've got physical evidence on the kid, but nothing else adds up." I caught my friend's gaze and held it. "I think they're going to hang this on LoDee, Charlie. I have a gut feeling he didn't do it. Call it a hunch, but he doesn't look right to me."

Charlie looked down at his paperwork and shuffled it. I knew he wanted to talk about something else. I paced across the room and back.

He raised his eyes to look into mine. "I miss seeing you in church, Jude. Why don't we talk this out?" He gave me a hug.

But I wasn't ready; I didn't think I'd ever be ready. The killing of Orval Miller fueled my anger with God. It appeared to me that God wasn't finished poking a stick into this angry bear.

I went home and picked at some old Chinese food from the fridge then went to bed early. My emotions had drained me. Besides, we had a long day tomorrow tying together the evidence against a kid I didn't think did the crime.

CHAPTER 6

Abdul, Ebdullah, Hamid, and Khaliq had risen from their morning prayers. As the four rolled their prayer rugs and prepared for the coming day, they talked quietly. Not that anyone was near the run-down former-mechanic's garage on the north side of Pittsburgh. They were quiet out of habit.

"When does Rafi return, Khal?" asked Abdul.

Khaliq closed his computer after checking the shared email account. As usual, he had left a saved draft instead of sending the message. Others on the shared account would check in and read it. He smiled to himself at the simplicity of their system as he slid the laptop into its sleeve. This way, they left no electronic trail to be traced by Homeland Security.

Khaliq yawned. "Excuse me, brothers, I was up very late last night cleaning up a problem." He stifled another yawn. "According to Rafi he will be delayed for another day." He shared the bad news from the most recent message with the others. "But he will come bearing gifts for the Great Satan's government."

Smiles broke out on everyone's faces at the thought of what those gifts would be: materials needed for the event they had traveled so far to accomplish. It would be the culmination of their training over the last ten years: the moment they had come to Pittsburgh for.

Ebdullah spoke. "It is good to know Rafi is safe, but his delay concerns me. He is our leader, and we can't do this without him."

He picked up his keys and headed toward the door for his rounds at the school bus center. "My little kiddies await me, and today I'm playing a new game with them on the bus. I might even sneak in a piece of candy or two before they arrive at the schoolyard."

"You spoil those kids, Eb. I think you are beginning to like them." Hamid shook his head.

"I do like them. Their minds are so alive and creative. It makes me miss my family in Afghanistan." Ebdullah's smile disappeared.

Khaliq turned away. Ebdullah may have left an eleven and twelve-year-old son and daughter at home, but they had all left family.

Ebdullah coughed. He gripped the key in his hand. "I miss my family, but they know I am a holy warrior. When we strike our greatest blow to the head of the Great Satan, they will be proud of me." He dropped his chin to his chest. "I pray to Allah that my son will follow in my footsteps and will understand what I do now." He turned toward the exit. "Until I see my own children in paradise, I will enjoy my little infidels and have some fun with them. See you all later." He pushed open the door and walked into the morning sunlight.

"What's on your agenda for the day, Hamid?" Abdul asked.

"Same as always. I mop up kids' vomit and clean up their spilled milk at lunch. Same old, same old," Hamid answered.

He sounded more American with each day. His ability to smoothly fit in made him the perfect choice for the school janitor position that their contacts had prepared. Each of them was getting good at blending in, with their non-Arab looks and English skills perfected over many years.

"Do you have your tools for this job in place?" Khaliq asked.

Hamid smiled. "Of course. Allah has guided my hand. Gotta run, fellow Holy Warriors. Vomit can't wait." He pushed the door open.

Abdul and Khaliq sat down, facing each other across a small table. Abdul's face showed the stress of the coming events. "Khaliq, are Rafi's problems going to change our plans?"

Khaliq shook his head. "Not at all. The package was delayed in Mexico City. The supplier wanted more money when he realized it was going to the mujahideen. It is okay in their minds to kill for profit, but sacrificing ourselves for the prophet Mohammed demands more money. Rafi is simply selling off the last of our interests in the heroin traffic in Mexico. The Islamic State is assisting with the rest of the funds and is helping with the transport. He will be on the road later today." Khaliq paused. "Do you have everything ready for your role in our holy war?"

At this, Abdul smiled. He had been a leader in the Taliban army in Afghanistan. His part was easy, something he did well — maybe the only thing he did well. "Khaliq, I am set and ready."

The two stood and embraced.

"My brother Abdul, in a few days we will see paradise," Khaliq said.

CHAPTER 7

Good morning, Mom." I slipped into her room at the nursing home.

"Is it time to go home?"

"No, you are home." I took a guess at what alternate time her mind was visiting at the moment. "You said you like it here at the school."

"Why in the world do you think I want to go back to school? I'm not learning a thing. Yesterday they tried to teach me how to be a waitress. I don't like kitchen work. Jude, I want to go home," Mom said emphatically. Her drift from one time zone to another was frustrating to me, and her latest visions of Miller and my Dad had stretched my patience. Yet there was something very strange about her latest dream.

I had to pull out the big guns now. "Mom, it would disappoint Zach if you left. Remember, he bought this school, and your dad paid for this room. It would disappoint them both." I told her flat-out falsehoods, but as long as she drifted through whatever she experienced as truth for the moment, I'd just as well try to use it to our advantage.

Mom sat back and reached for the can of Ensure on the table next to her bed. I waited for the Yoo-hoo story, but she must not have been in the mood. She looked at me with the eyes and the stare I remembered from my childhood. It was good to see it back.

"I heard about Orval last night at dinner," she said. "Don't believe anything you hear, Jude. I know there is something fishy." Mom's lucid statement and insightful thought stunned me.

"Why do you say that, Mom?"

"I was telling King Solomon about what happened, and he said—"

I threw my hands up like a cop directing traffic and strained to keep from laughing. "King Solomon? Like from the Bible?" Inside I laughed so hard I almost didn't get the question out.

"Yes. Now don't interrupt your mother, dear." She wagged a finger in my direction. "I was telling him about my visit from Mr. Miller and your dad. Then I started talking all about Mr. Miller's work with the kids in the neighborhood. I do enjoy talking to the king. He is as wise as your father was. You should have heard what he said." She sipped at her Ensure. I knew better than to ask, so I sat and waited. She would begin again when she was ready.

Mom fumbled with her slippers and told me all about how George, her fictitious friend from Germany, had sent them. I nodded politely and waited for the conversation to come back around to King Solomon. Impatiently, I prodded a little. "Proverbs is a great book in the Bible, isn't it, Mom?"

"The king shares so much wisdom in that book." To my astonishment and surprise, the prodding actually worked. "He listened to my story of Mr. Miller and said something was fishy. He leaned back and stroked his beard as he thought about it for a while." She imitated the motions. "Then he told me to tell you to read Proverbs 10:2."

"Why would King Solomon want me to read Proverbs 10:2?" I shook my head. Another message from another dead man.

Mom shrugged. "I don't know, Jude, but I would listen to him if I were you. Myself, I need to be careful of that man. Do you have any idea how many wives he has? I have no intention of becoming one more." A yawn almost swallowed the last couple

30

of words as she closed her eyes.

It was time to go, but her last statement allowed me to leave with a smile on my face. Wait until I tell Zach that Mom has a new beau.

As I slid behind the wheel of the SS 396, I considered whether to bother looking up the Proverb. I wished I had listened to my dad when he told us two boys to read a chapter of Proverbs every day for the rest of our lives. He said it was a book about character and, if we listened to Solomon's words, we would develop good character and be able to recognize the Bozos in this world. I chuckled at the name Dad called foolish people. I don't suppose the ginger-haired clown would have liked being portrayed in that light, but I wouldn't argue with my father for the civil rights of a clown being profiled simply because of the color of his face-paint.

With no Bible at home or at work, my familiarity with God's word had slipped drastically in the past few years. I needed to pick up my old Bible from Charlie's office. He had grabbed it from the garbage bin when I was throwing it out a few years ago.

I headed over and walked right into his office.

"Back again, Jude. Ready to take me up on my basketball coach offer?" His light-hearted word didn't match his dark expression.

I shook my head. "No, not yet, but keep working on me. You have the recruitment techniques of a Jedi Knight. My father has taught you well, Obi-wan," I joked as we shook hands. "Right now, I need to borrow something."

"Yeah, sure. Anything." He poked his head out into the hallway, looked both ways, then shut the door. "Whatever it is, though, we need to do it quickly, and then you need to get out of here."

Not quite the same reception I received yesterday. I gave him an are-you-joking kind of look, but his expression didn't change.

"What's wrong, Charlie? This isn't like you at all."

"After you left yesterday," Charlie spoke as if the walls had ears and the hallway operated like megaphone, "the Right Reverend B. A. Lamb swung by my office. He gave me specific instructions to not talk to you about Deacon Miller or give you any information. He said it was a police matter, and I was to stay out of it."

"I am the police, Charlie."

"Well, you ain't the right police, I guess. So, I can't tell you anything," my old friend stated, with a perplexed look in his eyes.

"Do I have to beat it out of you with a rubber hose?"

"Nope, just agree to coach a basketball team when all this has blown over." He smiled; Charlie knew he had me.

"Agreed. So what do you think made Lamb come to you and say that?" I asked as I slipped back into my cop persona.

"No idea. But there is something going on here. I will keep my ear to a drinking glass and that glass to the wall. This has sparked my interest, too. Anyway, you came in with a question. What can I do for you?"

"I need that old Bible of mine that you picked up from my garbage can." It was difficult for me to admit. "My mom said she met with King Solomon last night and he gave her a verse from the book of Proverbs that I was to read. My Bible is more comfortable to me than one of those phone apps." I said it as if my mother's dinner date with a long-dead Biblical figure was as normal as me having a doughnut while on duty.

Charlie just snickered. "You know this is crazy. I am talking to someone who could get me fired, for a reason I don't know, and we are talking about his mother having dinner with King Solomon."

"I figured it was time to reacquaint myself with that book, and I couldn't resist the urge to give an old friend a hard time. Besides, I thought you'd be happy I was showing an interest in something religious."

Charlie snatched my old King James Bible from his bookshelf. "What verse?"

"Solomon said to read Proverbs chapter ten, verse two." He flipped the pages to Proverbs and traced a finger down the page. "Ill-gotten treasures are of no value, but righteousness delivers from death."

I blinked. "What does it mean in light of this pending case?"

"Hey, you're the cop, so you solve the mystery." A shadow moved across the window of Charlie's office door. Charlie's eyes flashed fear, and he froze in place. "I'm sorry, Detective, but I can't help you." His voice echoed loudly enough that anyone in the near wing of the church could hear. "I know nothing, and I would appreciate you keeping me and my ministry out of your investigation."

He stepped to the door, opened it and motioned me out.

Reverend B. A. Lamb stood in the hall, just outside the door. He frowned at me as I passed him, but said nothing.

I quickly slipped the Bible into my coat pocket. I felt a little odd and a lot nervous, like I was smuggling a Bible out of a church. "Good morning." I nodded to the reverend.

"Jude Cameron, I am the Reverend B. A. Lamb." His cold tone didn't match his outstretched arm. "It would be nice to see you in church during our regular Sunday service hours. Maybe you can stop by then and limit your personal visits with my assistant."

I took the hand and shook it. His grip was cold, clammy and weak. My dad never would have shaken like that. Reverend Doctor Joshua Cameron said that a man makes sure the other guy knows he's a man when shakes his hand. Now I understood what he meant.

CHAPTER 8

When I strolled into my office, Captain Seeger and my partner stood next to my desk. The Captain looked up, and without any hello to precede it, said, "Cameron, in my office, now."

This didn't sound good.

Mounds of paperwork covered his desk. I sat in one of his straight back chairs, designed to keep you less than comfortable for a minimum amount of time. Seeger wasn't the friendliest guy, and today was no exception.

He started talking without even looking up. "Jude, we have the shooter in the Miller case. You are off it as of now. I don't want you bothering people with questions. Stay away from the church. Stay away from the perp. Drop it and go back to your other cases. Leave it alone, and that is a direct order." He looked up and stared at me for a moment to make sure I got the point.

"I don't have a good feeling about this case. I think there's more to it—"

"You're a cop. I am not asking for hunches, good feelings or bad vibes. I want results. The Commissioner wanted results and the Mayor wanted results. Ed got them, and that's it. Now get outta here." He ended abruptly with a jerk of his hand to motion me out of his office. I stood up and left.

The papers on my desk got the brunt of my anger. One stack of papers after another flew onto dusty areas of my desk. "Ed, what kinda crap is this? I'm a detective. I'm supposed to do all

I can to catch the real bad guys, and now I get pulled off a case that's flimsy at best, or a frame at worst." I grabbed another stack of papers and slammed them down.

"I think it is a done deal. In fact, the commissioner is giving me a promotion and a citation for solving this one so fast." Ed polished his nails on his old, circa '70's tweed sport coat.

"That's a bunch of bull, and you know it, Ed!" I thought I knew my partner better than this. How could he sell out his better judgment to get a citation and promotion? The answer rose without much further thought: retirement. With his upcoming retirement, a promotion meant more money. Was that what this was all about, money? This Solomon character my mom was talking to thought so.

I grabbed my keys and left without any idea of where I would end up, but my Chevelle took me toward Izzie's place. She might have dropped our romantic relationship, but that had been born out of our long-time friendship. I needed to talk to someone and didn't know who else would be willing to listen.

She answered her door with red eyes and a tissue in one hand, but attempted a smile. "What's up, Jude?"

"Your dad's case is taking some strange twists," I told her as I walked into her living room.

"My dad's case? That's pretty cold, Jude, even for you."

Her biting tone sliced through my anger. She was right. Once again, my cop-mode got in the way of a relationship. It had become too easy for me to separate myself from the emotions of a case. I shouldn't have brought this up with her. "Izzie, you know your dad meant a lot to me. I apologize for acting like a cop when you are hurting so bad, but this isn't about a case. This is about finding out what really happened, and making sure the right person is behind bars."

Her expression softened, and she stepped back from the doorway. "I'm listening, Jude," she said as she took a seat on the couch. I sat next to her. The sunlight cut through her cascading, deep brown curls, giving her a halo. She looked beautiful, and I felt like a fool for ever giving her up.

I explained my theory—as much as I could. I even told her about the message Mom passed on to me from the fictitious King Solomon. "I just can't find any other proof of LoDee's innocence. So all I'm left with is suspicions, but no idea where they're taking me—"

Izzie held up a hand to ask me to stop.

"You gotta let me finish, Izzie, because the verse she gave me, Proverbs chapter 10, verse 2 talks about ill-gotten treasures. As a matter of fact, the whole chapter is about the fool and how money will make him do crazy things."

She raised an eyebrow and crossed her arms over her chest. "Are you calling my dad a fool?"

"No, no, no. We both know your dad was no fool when it came to money. We both know he was as honest as he was faithful. This verse can't be about him; it has to be about someone else."

"So where is all this going?" She laid her hand on the sofa cushion.

My cop senses started to tingle. I sat on the edge of my seat. Maybe she had the information that would fill in the blanks so this all made sense. There was more to her story. "Izzie, I know that look. You've got a few facts or hunches filtering through your head that you aren't telling me. Was your dad in some kind of trouble?" My hands slipped down and grasped hers.

She pulled away from me and walked to the window overlooking the downtown Pittsburgh skyline. "I've had some suspicions, but I have no proof for what I am about to tell you. Take it like you would a conversation with your mom about Solomon."

I stood frowning. Instead of returning to the couch, Izzie fell hard into an oversized chair across from me. I dropped into the sofa opposite her.

She closed her eyes tightly for a moment before beginning her story. "About two years ago, Dad decided to do a major redevelopment on the last of the project buildings. He invested everything he had, and he was stressed over it.

"After the city council gave him the go-ahead and guaranteed the loans for the construction, they suddenly reversed their decision. Dad didn't know why, but I did. The new mayor had taken office and he wanted the redevelopment killed. Dad was hung out to dry. It nearly bankrupted him. He started selling off his other real estate, and that's when Reverend Amin came on the scene."

"The guy who started that group that wants to show how Christians and Muslims can work together?"

She nodded. "Right. They're called Co-Exist."

"How does he fit in?"

"Somehow he had enough money to buy half of Dad's real estate for a cut-rate amount. Rev. Amin owns the apartments, youth centers and more. How the head of a mission had the cash lying around to buy all those buildings, I will never know. "The part that puzzled Dad the most is that Amin somehow got the mayor to okay the redevelopment and also had the money for it. Word came in only a few weeks ago. That's about when Dad began acting paranoid. He was always looking over his shoulder."

Now she had me puzzled too. "Wasn't a Co-Exist group killed by a suicide bomber in Afghanistan?" I leaned forward.

"Yeah, nineteen kids died. It was so sad. My niece, Gloria, was in the group and miraculously survived." Izzie gave me her first smile of the last half hour.

"I had no idea about your dad's connection to Amin and the group of kids. Why didn't you mention this before, especially if it was making him act strange?"

"It wasn't Dad's proudest moment, and I didn't want to sully his reputation with you. He was crushed by the bombing. Over half of them were teens Dad got off the streets. They got pulled into Co-Exist because they wanted to do something that mattered in this world. But their deaths didn't put a damper on Amin. He has another group leaving for Afghanistan next month." Izzy gripped a pillow next to her as if to strangle it.

"Where did Amin come from?"

"I heard he had a church in Cleveland before coming here, but no one really knows. Dad had a private eye checking into it, but he died in a car accident on the way back from Cleveland."

I rubbed my chin as I considered the implications. "Lots of things seem to circle around this Amin guy." I asked another question that had just come to me. "Is there any link between Amin and our new pastor, Reverend Lamb?"

"Why do you ask that?" Izzie moved closer to the edge of her seat, staring into my eyes, seemingly anticipating my answer. I hoped my thoughts on Reverend Lamb didn't disappoint her. I filled her in on my encounter with the reverend. "By the time I got to the precinct, my boss was singing the same song. He threw me off the case and told me not to bother Charlie or you or anyone else involved." I pounded my fist on the arm of the couch. "I don't know how it fits in, but the more I hear, the more convinced I become that the verse from Mom's friend, Solomon, is on the mark, and ill-gotten money is behind your dad's murder."

"Amin came to town right after Lamb did. He started attending the church, and large donations were rolling in. Lamb appointed him as a deacon. I don't know who has their hands deeper in the other guy's pockets: Lamb or Amin."

I felt embarrassed that I had cut myself off from the church to a point where I knew nothing of their changes or politics. "There's a lot more to this." The pieces were finally falling into place. "We need to figure out what your dad wanted to talk to you about."

38

Izzie sat up straight. "If he had any suspicions, he surely had paperwork to back it up." Hope glittered in her eyes. She was on board with my hunch. I had finally found an ally in my battle for the truth.

"The question is, where did he put it?"

"That I don't know. My only other lead, clue, or whatever it is, came from my mother as well. I know this is craziness, but I have to follow this through. She said your dad came with my dad to visit her in the nursing home on the night he died. He told her to tell me the number two-fifteen." I shrugged. "I guess he thought I'd know what that means, but I don't."

Hands on her hips, she cocked her head to the side. "Jude, I can't believe you don't know what that is. That was Dad's old classroom number at the church, the one where we had our Sunday school classes in high school, where he taught us all the things we know." She snorted.

"We've got a problem then, since I'm not welcome in the building."

"You will attend the memorial service for Dad, won't you?" Izzie said with a glint in her eye.

I couldn't hold back a grin. "I guess he can't keep me from that. When did you schedule it?"

"It's in three days. That gives us plenty of time to come up with a plan." Life had returned to her eyes. This was the Izzie I knew most of my life. She was always planning and making things happen.

I gave her a hug before I left.

I had barely gotten to the street when I noticed a black luxury sedan with tinted windows parked across the street. No one put that kind of cash into a car except those who had money to burn — not the type of person who would live in this neighborhood. I could ignore it or like a good cop I could walk up to the suspicious driver. I chose the latter.

When I'd taken two steps toward it, the sedan pulled away from the curb. Its tires squealed as it shot by me. Before I could read the license number, the roar of another engine filled the air.

A red Mustang hurtled toward me. From the looks of it, it wasn't going to stop or swerve.

CHAPTER 9

I jumped back and stumbled up on the curb. The Mustang missed my feet by a fraction of an inch.

Someone was trying to keep me from looking any further into the case.

I would have to watch my back. Izzie would, as well. I picked myself up off the curb and brushed off the dirt from the street. I walked back to my car, checking every vehicle and every face. When I reached the Chevelle, I dropped to the ground and peered underneath.

Nothing looked out of order.

I unlocked the door with a quick jerk of my hand, then jumped back and covered my face with my arms.

Nothing happened.

I opened the door, leaned in to pop open the hood, and slowly lifted it. Maybe I'd watched too many cops and robbers on TV, or maybe it was my military training, but paranoia fully took over, and I checked for a bomb connected to the starter.

Still nothing.

I finally slid into the driver's seat. With rapid-fire fingers, I typed a text to my brother, Zach.

I need to talk to you right now. Where can we meet? Don't tell anyone.

The response came quickly.

DeMarco's Pizza shop, around the corner from my office.

I turned the key in the ignition, with a prayer that it wasn't waiting to take me on a heavenly journey. I pulled into a parking spot two blocks away from the pizza shop and performed every evasive maneuver I knew, just to be cautious.

Finally I slipped into the booth across from Zach. He had already ordered me an unsweetened ice tea and a couple of slices of pizza with just cheese. My brother knew what I liked to eat.

"Zach, someone just tried to kill me," I said in a hushed voice.

His eyes widened, and he froze with the end of the pizza hanging in his opened mouth. "Okay, big brother, what's the punchline?"

"No punchline. This is serious." I launched into the happenings of the last two days. Most of it took a few attempts to explain. "Now, here is the part that really spun my head around—until the Mustang almost took me out. Mom has a new beau. Unfortunately he is a few thousand years old. His name is King Solomon and, according to her, he is giving me verses in the Book of Proverbs to read."

Zach grinned at Mom's recent story. The part about King Solomon seemed to settle as easily as if I'd told him Mom got a new dress.

I finished by asking him to help me take Mom to the memorial service at dad's old church. "As I said, Reverend Lamb is not keen on my presence in the church, and Izzie and I need to search that old Sunday School room. Just try to cause a distraction for us."

Zach got a devilish look in his eye and said, "With Mom, that won't be a problem." He was ready to help in any way he could.

*　*　*

When I finally plopped down in my chair at the station, the late-afternoon sun slanted low across my desk. A message from the Captain lay right in front of me. It bore a simple message: I need to see you immediately.

I stood in the doorway of his office and stared at him.

He sat with his fists clenched, nostrils flared. "You've gone too far, Jude. You can't tell the difference between a direct order and following hunches. You've got this week off. And a whole lot more, I expect." He gestured toward my badge, then his desk.

I laid my gun and badge on his desk and stared right at him. "Something stinks, and I'm going to find out what it is. What are you afraid of?" I took a step toward him. "Why is this being driven by the powers that be downtown? I just hope you didn't get caught up in this as well."

He stood. "Take a second week as well, and when you come back we will have your disciplinary hearing. I'm asking that you be removed from duty permanently. In other words, I'm going to fire you if it is the last thing I do."

I jabbed my finger at him to accent my loud words. "I will find out who is behind this murder or die trying."

"You just might get what you wish for. Get out, and I don't want to see you again for two weeks." That ended the conversation. I walked out and drove home. I needed to pack for a little trip to Cleveland the next day.

CHAPTER 10

I disobeyed the Captain's orders. As soon as I got home I fired up my laptop and connected to the Internet. On-line detective work is no different than street detective work. You start with a word or phrase, then another, until a clue pops up. Then you follow that thread until another clue appears, and so on. You keep it up until the mystery is solved, hopefully.

It only took a few minutes to find the first concrete clue: a lead-in to an article from the Cleveland Plain Dealer. Several other hits led to the article, but there was one unfortunate problem: the article had been erased from the paper's server, or so it seemed when I got the 404 Error message. Either the Plain Dealer had gotten sloppy — which I doubted — or someone wanted to make sure the information contained in it was not easily accessible. If my churning gut could be trusted, then that full article would be enlightening to me and damning to Amin.

I was about to shut down the laptop for the night and get some sleep for my early drive to Cleveland when I struck on a new string of articles about Afghani attacks on humanitarian groups. Although none of the articles mentioned a particular humanitarian group, each one dealt my stack of clue cards another lead. There was an abundance of information but nothing that centered on the attack on the Cleveland church group. To get all the particulars and "drop-in" on that church, it would take my physical presence in Cleveland.

I closed the laptop and called it a night. Uneasiness crept over me, and sleep drifted in and out, mixed with images of my boyhood and the many trips years ago to the city that gave birth to my father.

I hit the road early the next morning for my ride to Cleveland, and I considered the warnings from both Zach and Izzie. Whoever killed Deacon Miller was more than capable, and ready to do the same to me.

I knew the journey well from childhood, but this time I drove with caution. I checked my rear-view mirror and quickly shifted lanes once I passed a semi-truck in the left lane. Two blocks later, I jerked back into the right lane, then turned onto a side road for a while. I was better at the stake-out-and-tail part of the cat-and-mouse game. Being hunted created a knot in my stomach that I wasn't used to. I tried to get my mind off the dangerous situation I found myself in, but it wasn't easy until I saw a familiar white barn along the highway.

During the many trips my family took to Cleveland, this dilapidated structure located twenty minutes after crossing the Pennsylvania-Ohio border marked the halfway point between Pittsburgh and my grandparents' home.

With a clear stretch of road in front of me, I turned on my radio to a Sportstalk station. They were talking about the upcoming Sunday game between the Browns and the Steelers. That was always a must-watch in my childhood home.

When it came to baseball my father loved the Pirates and Indians equally. He often prayed for a World Series between these two teams, but the baseball gods never heard his prayers. I could see my father sitting in his recliner, yelling frustrated comments at the umpires. Dad seemed so real to me in my memories.

Without any warning, I started to cry. Grief has a funny way of sneaking up on you. After three years, I still felt the pain of my father's loss as much as I did the day he died. I missed him.

He would have given me good advice on how to deal with this impossible situation.

I heaved a sigh so deep it seemed to come from the soles of my feet. If only I could have one last conversation with him. Before he passed away I never had a chance to let him to know what a great impact he had on my life. And I never told him I really loved him.

My emotional reminiscing came to an end as I pulled up to the large, ominous gray monument that read "Cleveland Public Library." I needed to research old newspapers for anything on Rev. Hussein Amin and his Co-Exist ministry.

My research of the library's digital archives yielded sore eyes and blurry print. I was getting nowhere. After one last stretch, I was about to take a break from the tedium when a headline caught my eye: LOCAL DELEGATION IN DEADLY ACCIDENT IN AFGHANISTAN. Now that sounded a little too familiar to pass by.

Eight local teens on a tour of Afghanistan were killed when their transport bus was struck by what is thought to be "friendly fire." A local pastor, Rev. Harry Aminton, led the group on a fact-finding mission. They were seeking ways that local Christians could build relationships with Muslim teens. In a brief interview with Rev. Aminton, he stated that "we were seeking ways to co-exist with Muslims when American weapons cut down their lives." Funerals for the eight students begin this evening at The Church of God's Peace....

Bingo! Too many similarities to the recent Afghanistan-related killings of Pittsburgh youths jumped out from the article. I printed it out and headed for the address in the article. Maybe someone at the Church of God's Peace could give me a lead or a clue. I needed some answers today.

The church was only a few blocks away. The area was run down, with more closed and boarded buildings than open ones.

Trash lined the streets, and the homeless and jobless coagulated on each decaying street corner.

I found the address, but it was another closed and boarded building. A sheet of plywood crossed over the front window of the former storefront church. If I wanted a lead, I would have to find it myself.

I parked a block away and walked around the back, to the alley and the rear door.

It had been pried open and offered no resistance. I pulled out my flashlight and personal weapon as I entered.

Holding my breath, I listened. No footsteps, no noise, no life. After I holstered my gun, I shined the flashlight about the room I entered. It was an old kitchen, and showed no sign of recent church potlucks.

I stepped over a spilled trashcan, and into what must have been the sanctuary. Only a few chairs that hadn't been taken for scrap metal remained, in front of a podium too large for where it sat. It was wide and ornate, with the church logo hand-carved into expensive cherry wood. I shook my head as I remembered what my dad would have said. "The sign of a small man trying to prove he is big in God's eyes."

I laughed to myself; Dad's beliefs had wormed their way deeply into my mind. My poking and lifting around the platform yielded nothing in the way of clues, so I moved toward the front door and the small front lobby, separated by a large window from the meeting room. My flashlight danced from dark corner to dark corner but exposed nothing of consequence.

I saw a thin, long table along one wall. Experience told me what I would find when I pulled its drawer open. That was where church ushers put the extra bulletins, and this drawer did not disappoint me. There they were—about three months of bulletins. I grabbed a few, folded them, and stuck them in my back pocket.

Light broke through open spaces around the plywood on the front window as I stepped back into the sanctuary. Something rustled in a corner. A mouse? An overwhelming sense of uneasiness settled around me.

I took a few steps back into the sanctuary when I noticed a moving shadow. I turned in time to see the butt end of a revolver coming for my head. The last thing I remembered was the floor rising to meet me.

CHAPTER 11

"My goodness, but the apple doesn't fall too far from the tree, Jude." My father said the words, but how could that be? He was no longer on this earth, so did that mean I was in Heaven too?

"Dad, is that you? Am I dead?" I tried to raise my head and open my eyes but I was still somewhere between out cold and awake. I lowered my head back to the cold concrete and drifted again.

"No, no, no." Dad's laugh echoed around me. "Not yet, but if you keep up the way you're going, then I'd better set a place for you at the table. You are tenacious. You get that from me, you know, along with your hard head. Although your head might not be that hard, or you wouldn't be lying here, bleeding on the cold, dirty floor of the Church of God's Peace. Where do these people come up with these names?"

I was beginning to think the blow to the head was really bad. I was also wondering how in the world my dad sneaked into my concussed brain. "I think I'm in over my head, Dad. Someone killed Orval Miller, and they are trying to hang it on a kid from your church. I need to help him, but I'm running into lots of blockades." I heard myself respond, but did I actually say the words out loud? How could I answer a dead man?

"I told Orval not to pull you into this, but he insisted. He trusted no one else to find his murderer or to protect Izzie. By the way, he is right that someone needs to protect both of you, and your brother, for that matter. These people are willing to storm the gates of hell from the wrong side."

"What do I do?"

"The same thing you've been told since you were born: Listen to your mother," he said with a chuckle.

"But Dad, Mom has dementia. She claims she has dinner with King Solomon every night and that you visit her regularly. She's not of sound mind any more."

"I guess talking to me is a sign of being a little wacky." He broke into one of his big barrel laughs that shook my body.

The loud laugh brought my eyes half open.

Dad got to his feet and leaned over me. "Wake up, Jude!"

He followed that with a slap to my face. Another slap jarred my loose brains back to the real world.

I opened my eyes to an unrecognizable face with a scraggly beard, only inches from my own. The smell of cheap wine on his breath confirmed I had returned to the real world.

The man shook me again and slapped me once more for good measure. "You gotta get up, mister. This place is on fire. We can't stay here any longer. Wake up!"

"Help me up." My head thumped like a horse stomped on me. Blood from my open wound flowed down my forehead and into my blurry eyes.

I knew I couldn't stand on my own. My savior pulled me up and threw my arm around his neck. We headed through clouds of smoke to the back door. Once we were in the alley, sirens swelled in the distance. Firefighters were coming, and that would also mean Cleveland police. They would call my Chief's office back in Pittsburgh, and that would not be a good thing. "Where does that alley over there lead?" I asked.

"The next block over. I'd take you, but everything I own is stored in that building. I have to go back."

"Is it worth more than a hundred bucks and your life?"

"Nope." His response came swiftly.

"I'll give you the hundred dollars when we get to the next block."

My homeless friend continued to lead me down the alley with his steadying arm around my shoulders. I could see flames dancing on the roof of the storefront church as I stumbled through scattered garbage. The wind had shifted, and billows of smoke rolled over us. It was hard to breathe, but the smokescreen would also make it hard to see us, slipping down the narrow alleyway.

Once we were safely away from the burning building I fished in my pocket, pulled out a wad of bills, and handed over five crisp twenties, stained red with the blood that dripped from my open head wound.

He snatched them, smearing the crimson stain along the bills.

"Buy what you need first, then do what you want with the rest." I knew where a large portion of it would go, but he'd more than earned the money, and that was his decision, not mine. "I know you came into the building to grab your belongings, but did you see anyone come out?" I asked.

"I don't want to get involved." He looked away, and for a moment I thought I recognized an old, familiar profile. Then he turned back to me, not meeting my eyes, the brim of his ball cap pulled down to heavily shadow his face.

"I don't want you involved. I just need to know what the guy looked like. It would be worth another twenty to me to find out." I pulled another bill from my dwindling reserves and placed it in his hand.

"I didn't get a good look, but it wasn't a guy. It was a woman. She wore a black ski mask and burst out the back door and up the alley."

"How could you tell?"

He shrugged. "Chicks run different from guys. She ran like a girl."

51

"Was she a big woman or a small one? Tall or short?"

"A tiny thing. I was surprised to see you knocked on the ground. She must have packed a wallop." He laughed.

"Trust me, she did. Do you remember anything else?" I fished for my keys; the sooner I made it out of the alley the better.

"No, she was running fast and out in the street before I really understood what happened. I smelled smoke, so I went inside instead of following her." He scratched his hairy black and gray chin and looked at me quizzically. "I was kinda wondering why you were in there. Are you a cop or something?"

"More of an 'or something,' my friend." I thanked him for saving my life and headed up the block to my car. I had parked far enough away, just in case I was followed. I hadn't realized that my diversionary tactic would put me out of range of the firefighters already hard at work, but I was thankful for it.

The incoming rush of locals to watch the flaming scene gave me even more cover. The walk and the brisk air helped to clear my head. I wasn't in the best of shape to drive, but my options were few. I had seen a motel a few miles away. I only needed to get there.

Once inside the car, I had that fearful dread about turning the ignition key, but I couldn't call attention to myself and check for bombs. I prayed, "Lord protect me," and turned the key. I thought I heard Dad's laugh.

CHAPTER 12

I examined the old Church of God's Peace bulletins while in the motel. There was a picture of Rev. Aminton on each one, which I hoped matched the face of my current Rev. Amin. One of the bulletins was from his last service in Cleveland. The blurb said he was being called to lead a missionary organization that could reach across the world and bring peace to warring nations.

He might be bringing something, but I bet it wasn't peace.

I also wondered if he had a young woman working for him. If he did, I hoped he would bring her to the memorial service in two days so I could look her in the eyes. I wanted to see her shock at my living, breathing form standing before her, and I wanted to even the score. After a few hours' rest and a handful of ibuprofen, I felt good enough to drive and hit the road for Pittsburgh.

I decided to make a quick stop at the nursing home to see Mom. For some reason I needed the comfort after my long, strange day. As I walked in, she looked at me and said, "What happened to you? You look terrible."

"I just have a bad headache, Mom. I'll be fine after a night's sleep." I slipped into the visitor's chair and rubbed my aching temples. "How was your day? Did Dad stop in?"

"He doesn't usually come in the afternoon, you know. He is a very busy man in Heaven, always about the Lord's work. But today he visited just as I was getting ready for my afternoon nap." She leaned over and fiddled with some of the large gift bags sitting on the floor next to her bed. She kept her worldly goods in them, always ready to leave and go back to her normal life. Unfortunately, normal would never be a part of her life again.

"What did he say?" I leaned forward with more interest than usual.

"He didn't stay long." She plucked a notepad and pen from a bag that said 'New Baby' and settled herself back in the bed before she continued. "He said there was a pressing matter back home that he had to attend to." She looked at me with that knowing smile moms have when they know more than they're willing to tell.

"What did he mean by 'back home?'"

"'Back home' has always meant Cleveland, dear. Something important was happening there. So he left his wife and ran off to take care of the Lord's work in Cleveland."

I laughed, a strangled sort of chortle. Mom's statement was too close to truth for my own comfort. "Well, you know Dad; he's always busy saving someone." The pain in my head thumped harder.

"But he did say to tell you to be more careful in the future and don't forget to protect Izzie and Zach. I thought that was strange, but I didn't have time to ask him what he meant. I figured you would know, though." Then she smiled that all-knowing smile again.

I pressed a hand to my head, which thumped even harder. I was somehow trapped in a world ruled by dementia and didn't know how to get out. I decided to change the subject. "What did you have for dinner?"

"Crap." She folded her arms across her chest and glared at me as though I was the one who had served it to her. She then pretended to spit it all out.

"What kind of crap, Mom?" Maybe if I got her to talk, 'King Solomon' would have another clue for me.

She returned to pawing through her bags, as if I wasn't there. I twisted in the old Naugahyde chair, making small noises in hopes that she realized I was still in the room.

Mom looked up and shook a finger at me. "I know what you are trying to do, young man. You just want to know if I had dinner with my new friend, King Solomon. I don't plan on telling you a thing." She climbed back into her bed, the item she was searching for apparently forgotten. "You probably think I am too old to have suitors, but you're wrong. Your mom is still quite a hot tomato." The twinkle in her eye matched her loud, happy laugh as she sat down. "Your dad always said I was one hot tomato, and he wanted to make a sandwich."

"Too much information, Mom." But I couldn't hold back a smile at the thought of Dad saying that to Mom. He loved this woman with all his heart and soul. "Now what did King Solomon say?"

"Jude, what is going on? Your father and King Solomon both seem to think you're in danger. Are you?"

"Maybe. That's about all I can say. I'm trying to sort it all out, and your conversations with King Solomon help me do that. Did he have another message for me?"

"I almost forgot. He said you needed to read Proverbs 29:4." Her eyes drooped.

It was time for me to go home, so I wrote down the verse and said my goodbyes.

The cool night air slapped my face as I dragged my exhausted and aching body from the Baptist Home. The parking lot was darker than I remembered it ever being. I glanced at the light posts. The lights should be on; they were on a timer. And my senses said that meant trouble for me.

I pulled my weapon from its shoulder holster as I headed toward my Chevelle.

I approached my car just ten parking spaces away in the

visitor's lot, examining the surroundings. There was a lot of open space between me and the car. I was wary of leaving the safety of the corner of the brick building. I glanced back along the side of the home. The only spot where someone could hide was behind the garbage dumpster at the far corner of the lot. I couldn't see into the dark shadows and without thinking slipped closer for a look.

I was about to back away and return to the nursing home when I heard the crack of a rifle shot. I heard the whistle of a bullet passing my ear.

CHAPTER 13

I slammed to the ground and listened.

No steps slapped the concrete.

I began a slow creep toward the corner. When I reached the building, I tucked my body tight along the bottom of the wall and used the unlit parking lot and solid brick as protection.

I pushed up slowly into a crouch to get a quick look at the assassin near the dumpster. I listened intently. Someone was moving away from me, up the wooded and brush-covered embankment.

I leaped to my feet and scrambled to the dumpster. When the clouds parted and the moon shone briefly, I got a fast look at a wiry figure as it crested the steep hill with a rifle slung over its back. I couldn't tell if it was male or female, but I assumed it to be the same person who tried to kill me twice before in the last two days.

I was considering the climb up the hill when two nurses stuck their heads out of the back door. "What happened? Did someone get shot? Are you okay?" one asked.

"Fine, I'm fine. It was just a car backfiring. It even gave me a surprise. Nothing to be concerned about. Go back inside where it's warm," I told them with my best 'nothing-to-see-here' cop voice.

As they closed their door, a door off the kitchen just thirty feet down the back of the building opened and shut quickly. A man walked hastily toward the employee parking lot on the other side of the building. A car started, and the tires peeled through the employee parking lot onto the pavement.

Without thinking, I raced to my car and cranked the ignition. I punched my Chevelle in reverse, whipped it around, and bounced onto the road. The car in front of me was in a hurry, but it was no match for my old muscle car. I pressed on the gas and was soon behind him.

I knew I would get into a lot of trouble for what I was about to do, but I slapped my bubble light on the roof of the car and turned on my siren. The trouble would be worth it to get the driver's license and registration and ask him some questions.

As the driver pulled onto the shoulder I slid my car in front of his to make sure he couldn't whip around me and pull away. I approached with my hand on my gun. From the man's frightened expression, he knew I was serious.

"License and registration, please," I barked.

"Was I speeding, Officer? My speedometer said I was doing only a few over the limit." His voice seemed concerned and innocent as he handed me his paperwork with a shaking hand. I snatched it before he dropped it on the ground.

"Could you step out of the car, please, Mr. McCagg," I barked again after looking down at his license and reading his name.

"What did I do?" The fear returned to his eyes. That I liked; it meant I would get the answers I needed.

"Someone turned the lights off in the Baptist Senior Home parking lot so someone else could take a shot at me. One of the nurses said she saw you do it. That makes you an accessory to attempted murder. You're going to go away for a long time." I hoped my embellishments would scare out of him the information I needed.

"I didn't do it. I don't know what you are talking about." He argued with all the conviction of a guilty man.

I spun him around and forced his face into the car hood. I pulled cuffs out of my pocket and slapped them on him before spinning him back again. I got my nose real close to his. "Listen, buddy, you are real small potatoes in this attempted murder. I would be just as happy to let you walk so I don't have to do the paperwork, but you have to give me something worth my while if you want me to turn my head."

"I don't know why they wanted the lights off." A quiver shook his voice.

"Then why did you do it? Did they pay you? Did you owe a gambling debt? Was it for drugs?"

"I did it for my daughter." He responded with what sounded like the truth for the first time.

"How did it happen? Can you identify the person who approached you?"

"Not really; they sent my daughter. She got in with a bad crowd and started using heroin. She's been stealing me blind, but she's all I got left in this world, since her mother died." Tears pushed their way out of the corners of his eyes.

"How did they set this up?"

He drew in a shuddering breath. "My daughter came to see me last night after I got home from work. One eye swollen shut, the other hardly opened. She said her dealer and his crew beat her up, so I knew they were serious. They told her if I turned out the parking lot lights when they called, they'd cancel her debts. If I didn't, they'd cancel both of us. I had no choice. I love her. I was scared to death."

"Why did they ask you to do that?" I asked as I rubbed my jaw.

McCagg was sobbing when he answered. "She didn't know much but she mentioned that some cop was getting too close to their supplier and needed to be taken out. They somehow knew you came here often. I just had to do my part and everything would be all right for my daughter and I."

"Where's your cell phone?"

"Shirt pocket."

I grabbed the phone and looked at the incoming call list. Someone had called ten minutes before I arrived at the nursing home.

"Whose number is associated with this phone?" I held the screen so he could see it.

"My daughter's."

"What's her name, and where is she living now, Mr. McCagg?"

"All I know is that she's been in an old house on Bluff Street." He gave me the number. "Please try to get Mandy out, Officer." Desperation colored his tone. "I'm sorry for what I did, but if you're a dad, you know you'll do anything for your kids."

After I unlocked his cuffs, I glanced at the cell phone again to memorize his daughter's number. "I'll do my best to help your daughter, but you have to let the cops know when these sorts of threats come your way."

He promised to do it, then slid back into the car. After I passed his phone and license through the opened window, he slammed the car into reverse, pulled around me, and hurried away.

Now I had a few more clues but wasn't any closer to solving the puzzle. I needed to look up that verse in Proverbs, but the pounding in my head convinced me that it could wait until I got home.

By the time I walked through my door, my head felt like someone had twisted it in a vice. I double-locked the door and put a few chairs in front of it to make some loud noises if someone tried to enter. I switched off all but one of the lights and lay down on the couch. I picked up the Bible on my coffee table and flipped it open to Proverbs 29:4. "The king by judgment establisheth the land: but he that receiveth gifts overthroweth it."

I dropped into the only remaining chair at the kitchen table and reread the verse. Made me thankful to be raised on the King James Version or I would have never understood the passage. Even so, the meaning didn't become plain until I gave it a second examination.

Solomon was telling me that government officials were bought off. I understood that part easy enough. But finding someone willing to kill a pillar of the local community and then attempt to kill to a cop three times would not be easy. Killing a cop was serious business. Only a big prize behind it would be enough motivation. The government corruption must go very deep, and that meant some very deep pockets must be behind this.

I closed the Bible and massaged my temples. It would take more brainpower than I had available at the moment. If I tried to figure it out tonight, my brain would surely explode.

Maybe Mom would have another message from Solomon overnight and save me some agony.

* * *

After a night of fitful sleep, I showered and went over to see Mom before I ran down some of the leads from my discussion with Mr. McCagg.

As I walked in the Baptist Home's front door, several of the nurses at the front station dabbed at their eyes as though they had been crying. Most of them took it hard when one of their residents passed away, but I thought nothing more of it. I had almost passed the station when one of them said, "Mr. McCagg was such a nice man. Who would have believed that he had such a serious drug problem?"

CHAPTER 14

I turned back to the nurse's station. "Excuse me, but what happened to Mr. McCagg?" My head began to pound again.

"We're not allowed to talk about it," a blonde nurse with short, cropped hair answered. "Then again, Jude, you are a cop." She glanced at the others around her, but no one reprimanded her. "He died last night from a drug overdose—"

"But it doesn't make sense, though," offered an older nurse. "He never showed any signs of using."

"No marks on his arms or anything that would have indicated drug use?" I asked, even though I knew they'd recognize it. But half of me wished it was true, so I wouldn't have to admit that my actions last night had contributed to his death.

The younger nurse answered, "We know what track marks are—and withdrawal symptoms. He didn't have either. I gave him his flu shot last year, and the poor guy nearly fainted at the sight of the needle." She shook her head. "It just doesn't add up."

"It is so hard to know about people, sometimes." I lied through my teeth, then quickly excused myself and headed for Mom's room.

Mom sat in her bed, with her Bible propped up on her knees. She held a large magnifying glass only inches from the pages.

"Good morning, Mom."

"Hello, hello. Long time no see." She dropped the magnifying glass as she looked up. "It is good of you to stop by. Did you see my mom and dad as you came in? They were just here, and they would have been so glad to see how big you've gotten. How old are you now?" Her serious demeanor — no playful smile this time.

"Thirty-four." I answered, with an ache in my chest for all we would never share in these last years of her life.

"One of my sons is thirty-four. You might know him. He's a police officer." Her eyebrows furrowed and her gaze drifted off. "At least I think so. He doesn't wear a uniform. If he wore a uniform, he might have a girlfriend. And if he had a girlfriend, I might be a grandmother." She took a sip of her now-cold morning coffee. "Do you have any idea what this tastes like?" She scowled as she held out the cup to me.

"You've told me before, and I don't need to hear that kind of language from my virtuous, saintly mother." I lifted some clean clothes from the chair beside her bed and opened a dresser drawer to put them away.

"Oh, Jude. When did you come in?" she said as she stood.

I was glad to see a part of her was back with me. But just how much was? "I just walked in a minute ago. I was talking to your mom and dad in the hallway, and that delayed me."

"Jude, you know my parents are in Heaven. Why do you kid me like that?" She turned away, then spun around as fast as her ailing body would allow. "Oh, did you hear the bad news about that poor custodian, Mr. McCagg?" She leaned forward and lowered her voice. "King Solomon said it has something to do with the case you're working on."

I whispered back. "How would he know that?"

Mom laughed. "He's King Solomon, and he is the wisest man in the world. He knows everything. So, is he right?" She ended in a whisper.

"That's what I'm thinking. When did you talk to King Solomon? I thought he was your dinner date?" I stressed the word dinner.

"I believe that man is trying to woo me." A blush of color highlighted her cheeks. "But like I said, I am not going to fall for some man with hundreds of wives and concubines."

The way she dropped heavily on the bed mirrored the emphasis with which she refused to entertain King Solomon's romantic interludes.

"Does he keep them all here with him?"

"There's no room here at the school, but I think he keeps them somewhere nearby."

She stared off into space for a few moments, and then switched gears again. "But he did have something for you. I think it was a verse. Let me try to remember. It was right on the tip of my tongue." Calm as could be, she looked right at me and winked. "You know I wouldn't forget a verse. Remember when I worked every morning with you and your brother to learn your verses for Sunday school? I may forget what I had for breakfast, but I don't forget verses. King Solomon said for you to read Proverbs 12:17. Do you know that one, Jude?"

"I don't remember it." Embarrassment warmed my face.

"Let me quote it for you. 'He that speaks truth shows forth righteousness: but a false witness shows deceit.' What do you think it means?" Mom asked, in the same tone she used when she asked a rhetorical question when Zach and I were kids.

I gave her my best Sunday school answer. "People tell lies to deceive and to keep people from finding the truth. Liars are hiding something, and they will distract from what is true by getting people to focus on the lie." I considered my answer and recognized the point King Solomon—or whoever he was— referred to. "I guess I need to find the truth."

"Oh, I almost forgot," Mom added. "One last thing. King Solomon said you need to find Mr. McCagg's daughter. She needs help before she ends up at the coroner's office."

The last statement hit me like a two-by-four smack in the

middle of my eyes. How did he know what case I was working on, much less any of the potential witnesses' names? Even if this King Solomon dude had a connection at the station, he couldn't have found the information there, since I'm wasn't officially working at the moment. My head started to hurt again. Who was this guy? How did he know all this?

"Your mouth is hanging open, dear." My mom's voice brought my thoughts back to her room. "Why are you so shocked? You learned about King Solomon's wisdom a long time ago." Her eyes squinted and she gave me that mother-look. "You do remember that, don't you?"

I told her I did, but my thoughts had already returned to the case. I had forgotten my promise to find and help the girl. I had to get to the old house on Bluff Street. I promised, and good men keep their promises. But I had one stop to make first.

CHAPTER 15

On the south side of Pittsburgh was what we officers called a "spy shop." It sold listening devices, bugging apparatus, and what I needed the most, a sweeper to check for listening devices. It was time to find whatever listening and GPS devices must be on my car to allow my enemy to track me so well. It was the only explanation for how he — or she, if my homeless rescuer was right — could have known I was on my way to the nursing home last night.

I walked through the front door of the old building and glanced around at this slice of techno heaven. Movement in the back of the store caught my eye. I saw the owner. "Rich, old buddy, I need a big favor," I said with a large smile.

"Well, if it isn't Mr. Former Cop." He smiled back, but it didn't reach his eyes. It was all about business with Rich.

"News travels fast."

"They always try to hang the honest cops early in their careers. The bad apples are the only ones who make it to the top." He shook his head. "I was sorry to hear about your troubles. How can I help?"

"I need to have my car swept for bugs and trackers."

Rich ducked behind the counter and came up holding his Spy Hawk Pro, the best bug detector in the business. He held the device out to me. "You know" — Rich twirled the gadget in his hand — "this little baby is only $350. I think it may be time for you to invest in one."

"Rich, I don't have that much spare cash, and you know my charge cards would be a dead give-away for my location this minute."

He sighed, nodded, and followed me out to the parking lot. When Rich scanned the device along my car, lights on it lit up like the proverbial Christmas tree. He found two devices on the Chevelle. One was to hear everything I said, and the other was a GPS tracker.

He shook his head and tossed the Spy Hawk Pro my way. "Keep it and pay me when you can."

Rich showed me how to turn the unwanted devices on and off with a remote control device that I did pay for in cash. I needed a way to lose my assassins or lure them when the time was right. I wanted my killers guessing all the time, and I didn't want them warning the drug dealers on Bluff Street. My only hope of getting in and out of that house with Mandy was a loud, big, and bright surprise.

It was still midmorning when I identified the dilapidated structure on Bluff Street and parked across the street and down a few houses. I first checked the empty street. No one was watching. I went to the trunk and pulled the blanket off my private collection to select what favors I was bringing to the party. Putting my bulletproof vest on first, I then put a flash-bang grenade in my pocket so I could shed a little light on the situation and stun those inside long enough for me to make it in and out without confrontation. Another revolver went in my trouser waistband, and I slung a shotgun over my shoulder. This cop was going in fully loaded. I half hoped I could use the fireworks and half hoped there would be no need for them.

A ski mask and wrap-around sunglasses finished my assault outfit. My stint as an Army Ranger came back clearly. Then I laughed. I was starting to enjoy this rogue cop persona I had adopted. I was finally in touch with my inner "Dirty Harry."

If the residents of the house I approached kept to the typical crack house routine, they would have been stoned all night and now would sleep the day away. My plan counted on it.

Kicking the door open, I pulled the pin on the flash-bang grenade, tossed it inside, and pressed my body against the outside door jamb with my eyes shut.

It exploded with an intense light and a horrendous bang.

With the sunglasses to protect my eyes, I rushed in with my shotgun under one arm and my Glock in my other hand. "Everyone down on the floor! This is a raid! Down on the floor with your hands behind your head." While their eyes flashed alarm, their bodies responded slowly to my commands. To encourage them to move faster, I fired off a shotgun shell into the ceiling.

Suddenly, everyone moved in a rush. One after the other, they hit the floor.

"Hands behind your heads!" I barked to remind their sluggish brains of the second part of my command. I glanced at the girls quickly, but none of them could be Mandy. If her dad was right about the beating, she would have facial bruising or a swollen eye.

I took the steps to the second floor two at a time. My best weapon was the element of surprise, so I needed to find Mandy as quick as possible and get out, hopefully before anyone realized what happened.

Halfway up, a guy with his pants hanging halfway down bounded onto the stairs. He stopped when he saw me and went for where his gun was supposed to be.

"Go ahead, make my day." I laughed at my own joke. I trained my Glock on him, and he slowly lifted his hands. "Back up the way you came. Any noise out of your mouth, and it will be the last thing you ever say."

The man turned around and retreated back up the stairs. When he stepped into the upstairs hallway, I smacked his head with the butt of my Glock.

His limp body crumpled to the floor.

I found Mandy slumped on the floor with her hands tied to an old radiator. I cut her ropes with my Strider SMF knife left over from my military days.

Her eyelids flickered, and she opened her eyes as her hands fell free. "Who are you? You can't take me. They'll kill my dad." Mandy attempted to scoot away from me, but her bindings gave her little room to move.

I took her by the hands and pulled her up. "I'm sorry, Mandy. I'm afraid they broke their promise. But I need you alive, so you're coming with me." I swept her up into a fireman's carry and headed for the stairs.

When I reached the top, I stopped at the sight of another gangbanger at the bottom of the stairs. I shifted Mandy's weight so I could aim my Glock and put a shot just above his head.

As intended, the bullet ripped through the closet door behind him.

He eyed me defiantly but backed away.

We hurried passed him, back through the main room. Most of the junkies remained where I'd left them, but one yelled after me, "You don't know who you're messing with! The boss's an important guy."

My body stopped and I faced the boy in a wife-beater t-shirt and baggy jeans. I raised my Glock and aimed between his eyes, speaking slowly and in a low voice. "Tell your boss something for me. Tell him a cruel messenger has come, and as the Good Book says, 'Vengeance is mine, sayeth the Lord.'"

CHAPTER 16

"Zach, I need a big favor." I glanced at Mandy, passed out on the back seat of my Chevelle. "You mentioned a rehab center for addicts that one of your clients owns. Could tell me where it is and let them know I'm bringing them an injured girl on crack? Make sure they know this is totally hush-hush."

"Good morning to you, too, big brother. Are you going to be finished with this in time to make it to our meeting with Izzie at noon?"

I paused before shifting the Chevelle into gear, then headed away from the crackhouse. As much as I wanted to speed away, I kept it under the speed limit. A ticket right now would not be a good idea. "What meeting? What are you talking about?"

"I see you didn't get the message—"

"I haven't been home much the last couple of days."

"We need to go over our plans for Orval's memorial service. You need to be at Izzie's around noon."

"Yeah sure. I'll be there, but I've gotta run. Now where is that rehab center?" I pulled up to a stop sign and waited for the address so I knew which way to turn.

As soon as he rattled off the address, I punched my foot on the gas pedal. Mandy was the only witness I had so far, and I honestly didn't know what she would be a witness to, but I was running on gut feelings.

By the time I dropped her off and got her settled, I had to

70

hurry to make it to Izzie's by noon. I rode up in the elevator, thinking about all that happened since Orval's death. How would I explain the details of the last few days?

Izzie answered my knock immediately. She barely opened the door before she said, "You don't look good."

"I've heard that a lot in the last few days. Is Zach here yet?" I walked in and pulled the Bible and the Church of God's Peace bulletins from my overcoat pocket and put them on her dining room table. I was so wrapped up in what I was doing I'd forgotten Izzie could have used a thoughtful, caring heart. I couldn't make that mistake again.

I stopped myself, took one of her hands, and looked her in the eyes. "How are you doing today? These plans for the memorial service must be tearing you up inside. What can I do to help?"

She pulled her hand out of my grasp. "You're already doing it. Just find out who killed my dad and why. That will give me closure."

Another rap at the door announced Zach's arrival. Minutes later, we all took seats around her table. "All right, Jude. Let's hear everything that happened," Izzie said.

I was well into a ramble about the preceding events, when my accountant brother held up a hand. Zach rubbed his temples like he did when we were kids and I would start rattling off the day's events. "Jude, you need to go step by step. It's like a math problem. We need to find out what we know so we can figure out the unknowns, or at least guess at them. Think algebra or trig."

"That's why you're the accountant, Zach. I may have barely got through basic math, but I understand what you're saying."

I backed up to the beginning of my story, about ready to summarize all the facts and my hunches when it struck me that I hadn't checked Izzie's place for electronic bugs.

I stopped mid-sentence and said, "Hold it." I wrote on a piece of paper, We may be bugged. Has anyone been in your apartment?

Izzie nodded. "Oh, I forgot to tell you, Jude. Your partner, Rivers, stopped by with another man. My instincts told me he was one of those full-of-himself young lawyers. He said it was routine to question family members. While Ed questioned me, the other guy walked around. That unnerved me a little. Do you think I may be a suspect as well?"

I nodded. "That's standard operating procedure. But Ed is sure that Lorenzo Deets did it." I grabbed the SkyHawk Pro from my coat pocket and began to sweep the room. It didn't take me long to find a device on the bookcase in the living room. "Hey, Iz, do you mind if I put on some music? I need to break the tension that has my back in spasms."

Izzie laughed. She knew exactly why I made the request. I moved the device to a spot in front of her Bose Wave radio and turned on the music. They wouldn't hear another word we spoke. But a nagging voice inside asked if we hadn't already given them enough. Why hadn't I thought to use the bug sniffer sooner?

We began the summary process from the beginning. Each of us stated what we knew.

"Okay, we know my dad visited your mother and left the message: 215, which refers to his room at the church. We can assume something is there, but finding it is tomorrow's job," Izzie said. "I already figured out how we can do it without arousing any suspicion."

"We also know that Lorenzo Deets was a disciple of Deacon Miller," Zach added another layer of facts. "And he sold his gun to the Deacon's gun buy-back program." He stopped and addressed his next question to me. "So how did someone else get his hands on Lorenzo's gun? Aren't the police supposed to destroy them?"

I nodded. "I've been thinking that one through. Either someone grabbed the gun at the buy-back, or we have a dirty cop in the evidence room. I've got a list of cops, politicians, and citizens who were at the buy-back. They are Izzie's dad, Reverend Amin, B.A. Lamb, someone from the mayor's office, and our ever-loving Captain Seeger."

I went on. "Now for the new stuff." It took me ten minutes to go over the events in Cleveland. As I finished detailing that part, I handed them each one of the bulletins I picked up from the church.

Izzie pointed to a picture on the back of the bulletin. "This Rev. Aminton is our Rev. Amin. No question." She shook her head. "I don't like the guy, but it's hard to believe he'd be involved with teens getting murdered in Afghanistan."

"Why does Afghanistan play such a big part in this?" Zach asked. "Is Amin a terrorist?"

"That wouldn't be my guess, but I really don't have an answer." Izzie wrapped her arms around herself and shivered, as though the thought had brought a cold winter's breeze.

"I'm beginning to think this Amin guy is dirty on a bunch of levels." I picked up one of the bulletins and examined Aminton's/Amin's picture. "Your dad must have discovered something that cost him his life."

Izzie stared out the window for a minute as she reflected on what I had just concluded. "You're right. What other clues do we have?"

"We have the verses from King Solomon...or whoever he is," I reminded them. "There's Proverbs 10:2, which says, 'Ill-gotten treasures are of no value....' From that, I assume money is the root of this evil and that money is coming from illegal sources."

Izzie added, "Then you have Proverbs 29:4. 'The king by judgment establisheth the land: but he that receiveth gifts overthroweth it.' We know someone has bought off political leaders and officials."

She tapped a finger on the Bible I'd brought with me, then

offered, "I've often wondered why some of the most ridiculous ideas and plans were approved by the city council." She shuffled the bulletins in front of her. "I'll do some digging around and try to figure out who was bought off. I have a friend at city hall, Cal, who can help me get to the bottom of this."

"There's a money trail in the midst of all this." I nodded to my brother. "Can you find it, Zach?"

"I would need to have someone hack into several bank accounts. Anyone know a hacker?"

"We'll dig one up," Izzie said.

She thought she might know a hacker? Strange, I thought, but then again, she had been an attorney.

"I forgot to tell you about one more incident." I leaned forward with my elbows on the table. "Actually, I didn't forget; I just didn't know how to say it. While knocked out in Cleveland, I dreamed I was talking to Dad. He warned me that I had to watch over you two, because your lives are in danger also. I would have just passed it by, except King Solomon told Mom the same thing." I pointed to Zach. "I think you ought to have Meg and the kids go stay with her mom in Buffalo for a few days. That way they won't get in the way if the killers go after you."

"Great idea, except for one thing: who's going to protect me from the killers if they come after me?" Zach grinned as though he was joking, but a hint of fear glinted in his eyes.

"I'm working on that, little brother. I'm working on it."

Izzie laid out the plan for how we would get to her father's old Sunday school classroom tomorrow without suspicion.

I leaned back and nodded. It was a good plan, but nothing seemed to be going as planned in this case. I couldn't help but wonder what would go wrong with this one, in spite of all our detailed preparations.

CHAPTER 17

Fifteen minutes later on the road, a new, red Mustang fishtailed around a corner and took up residence behind the Chevelle. My tail was back, and it was time to have some fun. Pittsburgh and its surrounding area was my town. Like any car-crazy teenager, I knew all the streets. Every twist, curve, rise, and fall of every road.

I led the Mustang onto the ramp for I-279 and headed north. There were a few things I needed to school my tail on when it came to Pittsburgh. When I hit a stretch that local cops did not police often, I slid easily into the open passing lane, then punched the gas pedal until the needle on the speedometer hovered over the one hundred and twenty mark.

The Mustang wove in and out of traffic in an attempt to keep pace with my Chevelle SS 396. The driver must have felt he or she was doing a fairly passable job, but obviously didn't know the potential of my performance-enhanced Chevelle, with its powerful 325 horsepower, 396-cubic-inch V-8 engine.

I jammed the gas pedal down again. At the last minute, I whipped into the right lane and onto the exit ramp for McKnight Road. I wanted to take this joker behind me on a real ride through Pittsburgh's winding hills. I'd see if the driver could keep up with me on my turf. Might it be the woman who clocked me in the head?

I slowed as I passed the shopping centers and hit typical

traffic in front of the mall. It was the kind of stop and go, bumper-to-bumper traffic that had given McKnight Road the nickname McNightmare Road.

Treacherous Ingomar Road was ahead on the left, and the Mustang driver would have the time of her life maneuvering that carnival ride. After I turned, I floored the Chevelle again. The Mustang stayed with me, rose and fell more times than a roller coaster but with tighter, more frightening turns. I had to give the other driver credit for keeping up. Then again, I wanted the car close.

I imagined her sweaty palms clutching the steering wheel as we hit tight turns at seventy-five miles per hour. I hoped the driver's heart pumped and her stomach tightened until she could taste the bile as we flew over one hill, then another. Several times my wheels left the ground, but I knew and anticipated every one of those airborne spots, and my enemy did not.

The other car stayed behind me until I took a hard right onto Brandt School Road. I waited until I was far enough ahead to pull into a small church parking lot. With my headlights off, I sucked in a deep breath and waited. The Mustang roared past me a minute later. It crested the hill, left the pavement, and banged onto the hard asphalt. Now it was my turn to play cat and mouse, only this time I was the cat, waiting to pounce. The driver would come to the red light in another minute, and that was when I would make my move. I slipped my Glock out of the holster and laid it on the seat next to me.

CHAPTER 18

Unless the driver of the Mustang knew the roads, when they pulled up to the light they would be unfamiliar with the lanes. That stoplight confused even born-and-bred Pittsburghers. The driver took the outer, left turn lane, heading toward the I-79 North ramp. I rolled up next to the car and pushed the button to lower my passenger's side window.

The Mustang's dark-tinted windows didn't give me a clear look at the driver, but inside surely sat a frustrated enemy. I raised my Glock as if ready to shoot.

The Mustang peeled out, running the red light, and was soon on the I-79 North ramp.

I laughed as I made a turn to head south, back to the city to make a call.

As I drove past Tom's Diner on West Liberty and turned into the parking lot, I glanced through the restaurant's large picture window. Sure enough, my old partner Ed sat at his usual table where he could watch the passers-by. His constant vigilance had saved both of us many times. I parked, strolled in, and took a seat across the table from him.

"I ordered you the gyro omelet and black coffee right after you called." He sipped from a cup, one of many cups of thick, dark coffee he would drink throughout the day. "So what brings you to this lovely little establishment?"

"I want some answers, and I want the truth."

"I think the kid did it. It's as simple as that. The evidence lines up. So quit busting my chops about it." He stabbed a piece of meatloaf with his fork and put it in his mouth.

"Don't you think it was all a little too easy? That all the evidence testing came back too quick? Those are signs of a set-up. There are some higher-ups in our department, or the government, who are dirty. Now, tell me why you went to see Izzie?"

He took another bite of his dinner before answering. "The mayor sent some boy lawyer over to the precinct. He didn't want her to say anything that would splash back on his royal butt. So I was ordered to take him to her place so he could ask some questions. That was it. Nothing special. All routine, except for that kid lawyer I had to drag along.

"What a pain he was. The kid never sat down. He paced the room, lifted books off shelves, and fingered her stuff. Isabella had a scowl that ran across her face every time he picked something up. Heck, I was perturbed, and it wasn't even my stuff," he said, between bites of his meatloaf.

"What else do you know?"

"They delayed LoDee's arraignment until after the service. They can't find a lawyer to take his case. No one wants to touch this one. The Public Pretenders are all out sick until next week. I guess Orval Miller was pretty well connected in the political arena."

I leaned back and shook my head. "And you still don't think there's anything unusual about this case?"

Ed set his fork down. "Listen, Jude, I wish it hadn't turned out the way it did for you. The chief is going to have your shield. You're finished with the force unless you lie low for the next two weeks, then go in and apologize. The Fraternal Order of Police lawyer says he can make it so you keep your job." He jabbed his fork in my direction. "I've been working for you behind the scenes, Jude. We're partners, remember?"

"I'll think about it."

A flash of red on the road outside the window caught my attention. I looked just in time to see a red Mustang pull into the parking lot. "Did I tell you there have been three attempts on my life in the last couple days?"

Ed laughed as if I was joking.

"I advise you to duck, because number four is about to happen."

Ed had enough time to get a glance at the figure in black as she rolled down the window and aimed a gun at our booth. We both dropped to our sides on the booth bench seat. I heard the crack of the gun, then the shattering of the window. Glass came down on us both in a twinkling shower of shards. Patrons screamed. Our waitress fell to the floor with fright in her bulging eyes as she let loose a gasp. I rolled my head to see if anyone was hit.

Everyone seemed fine but terribly frightened. Over the screams of Tom's patrons, I heard the Mustang burn rubber as she pulled out.

Ed leaped to his feet and took a step toward the door, but I grabbed his arm. "Don't even try. The Mustang is already gone." I stood and brushed the glass from his coat with my napkin. "You'll have to stay for the black-and-whites. As far as you know, it was a random, drive-by shooting. I've had a long day, and I'm going home to bed." As I strolled toward the door I looked around at the faces of the sparse group of customers. They were slowly gathering themselves from under their tables or off the floor. Their fear kept them preoccupied for the moment, their heads low.

I threw a sizable tip on the table and walked out without having touched my glass-peppered gyro omelet.

When I got to my apartment, I pulled out the SkyHawk Pro, held my breath, and did a sweep of my few small rooms, but found nothing. It didn't take long, my one-bedroom apartment had only enough furniture to make it look and feel like a bachelor's pad. None of my books or newspapers had been moved from their recent landing spots. The maid, if there had been one, hadn't cleaned in awhile.

After the search it was obvious that my pursuers had not been in my house yet. Surprising. Why would they bug Izzie's apartment and not mine? Disconcerting.

I sent her a text. Keep your doors locked and your Glock under the pillow.

She texted back. Already there.

I slowly undressed, feeling the aches of exhaustion in my muscles. I dropped onto the mattress without pulling back the sheet or blanket. I closed my eyes, but each noise on the street below popped them back open. When the stairway that led up from back of the building creaked with the weight of a body, I slowly slid from the bed, wrapping my hand around the butt of my revolver. I moved to the door and cracked it open to get a clear view of the hallway. The old man down the hall was returning from taking his dog for his last outing of the day.

A long sigh escaped my lips as I quietly closed and locked my door again. Shaking my head at my own paranoid actions, I laughed. When I hit the bed a second time, I pulled the pillow over my head to block out city noises and fell into a restless sleep filled with the fear of intruders.

CHAPTER 19

"Interesting place to meet." The man admired the long, black hair of the woman sitting on the steps with a sandwich in front of the Lincoln Memorial. A pity he wouldn't be able to enjoy such feminine sights once her people ushered the caliphate and its Sharia law into the country. Too bad, he thought. Nadeem was a beautiful woman. He sat a safe distance from her and looked away as if enjoying the view.

But he clearly heard her voice. "It is a fitting place. This memorial honors President Lincoln, who presided over the Civil War in this country. When our mujahideen attack the centers of moral corruption in Washington, we will see our fellow Muslims rise in a greater civil war. So this is a very fitting place to sit and reflect upon our holy war."

"The army will fight back, you know? The gun-toting Bible-thumpers will fight as well."

Her tone changed. "We understand the costs. Now, what is it that you want?" She spat the words.

He cleared his throat. "I need to make sure my position in all this is secure. I don't really care about your Sharia law and your caliphate. I just want to make sure my interests are protected. My people need a place in this, or I will not lead them to aid you."

"That is beyond my scope," she said. "I can only relay your message to my contact. What more do you want? I cannot make promises."

81

"Nothing more than was already promised. I am only wondering how your people plan to start this first wave of attacks. I need a sign that tells me it is time for me to intercede in Congress. I expect to be president, and I expect your buddies to drop that into my well-deserving lap."

"Believe me, you will not miss it. Have your people ready three days after the day of the Great Reckoning. Now, please, do not contact me again until after the beginning of the end." Nadeem wrapped up her sandwich, rolled up her brown bag, and placed it in her satchel. She stood and walked away, never looking at her stoop-mate.

* * *

Nadeem strolled in the cool, wintry air back toward the White House. She made a mental note to tell Habibi that this greedy American needed to be beheaded once his usefulness passed. Maybe she would slit his throat herself. The thought brought a tight smile. But others who walked freely throughout the halls of the White House would fall to the edge of her knife first.

Her mind drifted toward the recent news from Rafi, the head of the Pittsburgh cell, and his problems in Mexico. His delay would put pressure on the others to finalize the plans. He'd assured her that the package would be delivered on time, but she still had some concern. Khaliq was a resourceful leader in Rafi's absence, but Rafi was the one the terrorist cell looked to for spiritual guidance.

As she reached the crosswalk, Nadeem straightened her business suit, stiffened her spine, and proceeded to the unsuspecting White House.

She was a bright girl when she entered Harvard almost two decades before. There was no doubt during her years at the prestigious university that she would make her Afghan parents proud. They had come to America for freedom and to escape the oppression of radical Islamists — to give their daughter everything

82

they did not have while living in Afghanistan. How surprised her father would be to find out that his daughter was radicalized early in her freshman year by the same forces that he fled from.

Nadeem's brilliance in political and law studies made her more ideal as a sleeper than as an activist. She was trained to become exactly what she had become, an adviser to the president of the United States on Islamic affairs. No staff member or congressman would breathe any concerns about her without worrying that the protective world of political correctness would attack them. She was a woman. She was a Muslim, and she was close to becoming the president's chief adviser.

Shortly after Nadeem walked back into her office, the president's senior adviser stood in her doorway. "The first lady and I plan to kick back and watch a movie tonight. Do you want to join us? It will be late, and if you like, you can stay in my suite."

"A girl's night out. Sure. After being around all these alpha males every day, I could use a little girl time. When should I meet you?"

"Nine. Meet us in the theater room."

Nadeem didn't like the senior adviser, but the adviser liked Nadeem. It allowed her to make inroads into the backroom workings of the White House. Nadeem played every angle. She knew that information was power on the political stage, and each kernel of information made her more powerful. There was no one more powerful than the president's senior adviser. No one guided more decisions and no one held more information than she did.

CHAPTER 20

Morning came quickly, and my body wanted more sleep. Instead, I showered and put on my black suit for the memorial service.

Zach was picking up Mom at the Baptist Home. I was to wait outside the church to help him get her inside. Her stroke hadn't rendered her helpless, but it did limit her movements. Izzie's green Volvo sat in the parking lot, just outside the front door. Inside the foyer, she shook hands with a tall gentleman, then spoke to the couple who waited behind him.

I nodded to her as I passed. It was time to put our plan into action.

When Zach arrived with Mom, I met him with the wheelchair I snagged from the side room where they always kept several.

Mom grimaced at the sight of the chair, but settled herself in it without comment.

"Ready for the tour, Mom?" Zach rolled her chair toward the door that led out of the sanctuary into the Sunday school hallway.

A large, muscular usher in a black suit raced past them and blocked the doorway with his large body. "I'm sorry, but this is a restricted area. No one is allowed beyond these doors." But his hard expression said he was anything but sorry.

Zach started talking. "Sir, Mrs. Cameron, wife of the former pastor, just wanted to look at the rest of the church. Mom hasn't been here since she had a stroke. I thought she'd love to see the

Sunday school rooms again, since she taught in most of them." Zach words remained gentle, but issued a subtle challenge.

"The answer is still no. You will have to stay in the sanctuary."

Mom pulled on Zach's suit sleeve and when he bent down, she whispered in his ear.

Zach held out a hand and steadied her as she pulled herself out of the chair.

I hid a grin behind my hand and giggled inside. This young man was about to get dressed down by the toughest Sunday school teacher this church ever knew. She never abided disrespect in any way, and this young man would soon feel the sting of the Edna of old.

I edged a few steps closer so I could hear Mom do her thing.

She released Zach's arm, steadied herself on her own, then raised a long, arthritic finger before the usher's face, her slow wind up to the delivery. "Well, if it isn't little Paulie Johnson, all grown up. Does your mother know how disrespectful to your elders you've become? I suppose she does because you have not changed one bit since I had you in Sunday school.

"I can remember sitting with your weeping, broken-hearted mother and praying that God would change your dark little heart. I can see your dear, sweet, saintly mother's prayers were not answered."

The chastised Paulie flinched. "My mother passed away two years ago."

She clucked her tongue. "She would be very disappointed in you. All she ever wanted was for you to serve God. It appears to me that when the choice between serving God or Mammon came along, you chose the latter." She wagged her finger in his face. "Aren't you ashamed of how you have disappointed your saintly parents? I can still remember your father standing up in this very sanctuary and testifying. With tears in his eyes, he told about how he failed his family, but with God back in his life, he would move heaven and earth to change his wayward kids. I can see that heaven and earth might have been moved, but nothing has moved you.

"And I do believe that you may have forgotten that my husband built this church from a storefront to a community institution. If you would like to defame his name and character by your actions, then that is your decision, but I will respect his wishes that this church is open to all people, at all times."

She finished in dignity and asked Zach to help her sit again.

Paulie stepped aside and opened the door.

Rev. Lamb entered the sanctuary from his study and looked at them with a frown, walking toward my mother and brother. I thought it better that I not approach him.

Izzie must have been paying more attention than I thought. She caught my eye and nodded. She broke away from the young man she had been speaking to and hustled to cut the pastor off, delaying his progress.

Once Mom sat back in the wheelchair, Zach pushed Mom through the now-open doors to the Sunday school area, with the pastor stuck talking to Izzie.

Paulie said nothing as he held the door open wide, but several tears wet his cheeks. The Holy Spirit's work of convicting a soul through the words of a dynamic woman of God was powerful and not to be denied.

Rev. Lamb seemed to know when he'd lost the battle. Instead of interrupting, he settled into a discussion with Izzie.

I hurried to Izzie's side. It was the perfect opportunity for her to ask for permission to retrieve her father's personal items from his Sunday school room. I needn't have worried that she would miss the opportunity. As I joined them, the reverend answered just that question.

"I cannot let you do that. It is the church's policy that all items brought into the church belong to the church." He gave her a bright but insincere smile.

I snickered loud enough that he sent me a glare, followed by a sneer.

Izzie shook her head. "Reverend Lamb, I respect your opinion, but there is no legal precedent for such a seizure of personal property." She set a hand briefly on his arm. "These are items of sentimental value to me, and I will be picking them up. My suggestion is that you take me to court after my retrieval, and we let them decide who owns the materials." She turned to me and asked, "Jude, will you assist me in getting my father's things?"

I grinned from ear to ear. I loved it when she talked all that legal stuff. Sometimes I forgot she had been a successful lawyer before entering politics. "Sure, Iz, I would be glad to accompany you."

Paulie protested our approach to the open doors, but Lamb waved him off before heading toward his study. He had something in mind, and I knew it would mean danger for Izzie if we didn't move fast. Taking her arm, I escorted her quickly through the same door Zach and Mom had used and headed for the staircase to the second floor.

CHAPTER 21

Room 215 was locked, but Izzie fished through her purse and held up a duplicate key. She could have been a Boy Scout, the way she was always prepared. She pushed the door open and walked in slowly. How she kept from crying right then and there, I didn't know.

My eyes started to fill with tears as I took in the sights of a typical Sunday school classroom: posters of Bible stories on the wall, extra Bibles stacked neatly on top of the counter, a jar holding pens and pencils.

Then Izzie charged into action. She pulled open each drawer in the counter and dumped everything into a tote bag she drew out of her purse. "Grab the pictures from the walls, Jude. Dad loved to hide important documents behind them."

I had pulled three pictures down and stacked them on one of the tables in the middle of the room when I came to a calligraphy-style verse, Proverbs 2:3-4. "Izzie, listen to this verse, 'Yea, if thou criest after knowledge, and liftest up thy voice for understanding; If thou seekest her as silver, and searchest for her as for hidden treasures; Then shalt thou understand the fear of the Lord, and find the knowledge of God.' Someone underlined the words 'hidden treasures' with a felt-tip pen."

I pulled the framed scripture off the wall. "I think—"

A small-framed, wiry woman walked into the room. She had straight, black hair and wore tinted glasses. "I am Reverend

Lamb's secretary. He sent me to ask you to cease and desist your illegal activities." Her slight Middle Eastern accent triggered an unconscious memory from the Cleveland incident, and I knew I was looking at my attempted murderer.

"Tell him to sue me," Izzie snapped.

The secretary's face tensed, and she moved with an intent to physically prevent Izzie from cleaning out the desk drawers. She made the mistake of not watching me.

While the woman's focus centered on Izzie, it was time to even the score just a little. I used an old street basketball move, stepping in front of the woman with my back to her, and I threw an elbow designed to injure. On the court it would be a personal foul; in a Sunday School classroom, it was personal payback for ruining my omelet. My elbow crashed into her glasses, shattering them into her face, cutting her cheekbone, forehead, and around her eye. She crumpled to the classroom floor with blood dripping down her face and onto her crisp black suit.

Izzie stood, her back to the wall, eyebrows raised as high as they would go.

"I'm sorry," I told the woman without the slightest hint of sincerity. "I was just trying to get something from the wall and accidentally raised my elbow as you passed." I intentionally made my apology sound as fake as it was.

The woman wiped the blood from her eye. Her red-stained hand slipped toward a lump underneath her suit jacket. A bad choice I had to remedy immediately. My black dress shoe slammed down hard on her other hand, which lay palm up on the floor, a great target for a distraction. I heard bones crunch. The woman on the floor squirmed in pain and a shriek exited her grimacing mouth.

Her uninjured hand stopped. That gave me enough time to pull my gun and shove it in her face. "I just can't believe a virtuous servant of the Lord, filled with God's love, would have a gun under her coat, but if she were to use only two fingers to pull it out, I might not be inclined to twitch my trigger finger," I said with a fake smile.

With only two fingers, she pulled the gun slowly from her jacket and dropped it on the floor.

I kicked it toward the door, where I could pick it up when we left. Izzie finished packing her father's things as I trained my gun on the woman sprawled on the floor. The last thing Izzie did was take down the rest of the pictures.

I scooped up the stack with my free hand as I backed away from my would-be-murderer. I tried to memorize her face and offered some Biblical advice. "The scripture is quite plain, for the Bible says, 'Vengeance is mine, sayeth the Lord.' Think of me as God's cruel messenger the next time we meet."

I snatched her gun from the floor by the door before waving Izzie, with her tote full of her father's belongings, out into the hallway.

While Izzie would take her father's belongings home, I planned to have the ballistics from the assassin's gun checked against the bullet from Tom's Diner. In the hallway, Izzie shook her head as I took the heavily loaded tote bags from her. "You really know how to show a girl a good time."

She walked briskly back to the crowds gathering for the memorial service, and I headed to the parking lot to hide the bags and pictures in the lidded playground sandbox. I'd pick them up on the way out. By the time I returned, the organist had begun the first hymn. I made my way to my seat next to Mom.

Zach leaned across her and whispered, "What happened?"

"We did a little payback," I said with a big, toothy smile.

As the third hymn ended, I blinked in surprise. Rev. Amin stepped up to the pulpit and read the Twenty-Third Psalm. He did it with a grace and eloquence that would make one think he believed what he read. I could only think about the young people who lost their lives on their trips to Afghanistan. They had walked through the valley of the shadow of death, but their guide was the evil they should have feared.

After Amin sat down, the choir started to hum Amazing Grace. The director, Sister Hilda Hill, stepped to the microphone. "The choir would like to dedicate this song to Deacon Miller's memory, to his daughter Isabella, the Reverend Doctor Cameron, and to my oldest and best friend, Mrs. Edna Cameron. Most here and in the choir owe their Christian lives to the Camerons, these saints of almighty God. For without Doctor Cameron's amazing grace and willingness to share the gospel, we would not be here."

I remembered the choir as being rousing and exciting, and even in this soft and gentle rendition of Amazing Grace, power poured out with their voices. On the last verse, a girl in her mid-teens walked up to the microphone. The tempo and volume swelled as she began to 'testify in song' as my Dad used to call it when the singer began vocal rifts and runs. This singer was amazing.

Mom stood and clapped in sync with the song's solid bass line. Nothing laid down a solid bass like a Hammond B3 organ.

Zach tugged on her arm. "Mom, sit down," he whispered.

"Let her be," I told him. "This is church as she remembers it, and that is the way it should be."

Soon others stood and clapped. Mom yelled out, "Testify, testify!" The old familiar "amens" rose, scattered throughout the congregation. The sterility of B. A. Lamb's First Baptist Church disappeared, replaced by the spirit that had permeated the building throughout my formative years. By the time the song ended, everyone was standing and clapping except for the Right Rev. B.A. Lamb.

The air was still electric with the power of the song when Rev. B.A. Lamb stepped to the podium. I felt the energy escape the room like the air from a hissing balloon, and I wasn't the only one who felt that way. Something told me this wasn't going to be like my dad's sermons.

He spoke. "The Psalmist wrote, 'Though I walk through the valley of the shadow of death.' On my many walks through the neighborhood with Deacon Miller, no one here could have that same sense of peace as they walked through our neighborhood streets filled with our society's rejects. Deacon Miller had no reason to fear the valley of death or even a shadow in the valley of death. I once witnessed him wade into a crowd of gun-waving youths who threatened to kill one another. He stepped between them and asked which one would be willing to shoot him first to get to the others. They all backed away.

"That is the Orval Miller who helped establish this church, redeveloped our community, and won back those children drawn away by the evil forces of today's wicked society.

"We can all sleep better at night and be thankful that our heroes on the police force moved quickly to find and arrest the killer of our dear friend, Orval Miller.

"But there are still some who throw mud at the memory of Deacon Miller by refusing to acknowledge the identity of the true killer. Their seeking of false answers and lies has brought that valley of death closer and closer to their own doors.

"Pray that God will punish those who spread false rumors. In the book of Proverbs, King Solomon said that there are 'words of life and words of death.' Those who seek after 'words of death' will bring the wrath of the Almighty God down on them" — Lamb paused and pulled in a breath— "and their families."

Lamb was preaching hard. Sweat dripped from his brow, and he wiped at it with a neatly folded handkerchief. And all of his hard preaching was directed at me. Was it a warning or a prophecy? If he was speaking a prophecy, then everyone hearing it would not be surprised if I died in an unusual situation.

As Lamb made his points he smacked the podium harder

and harder with his open palm. I heard somewhere in the back of my mind my father's voice. "When you don't have a strong point, just pound the pulpit harder." Lamb was an audiovisual of just that statement.

Mom leaned over to whisper in my ear, "Your dad is right, you know."

"Right about what?"

"The pulpit pounding! Weren't you listening? He just said it."

I had heard it, but I didn't think Mom did as well.

The sermon ended. After the last hymn, we waited for the hundreds and hundreds of people to exit the building. We would be going with Izzie to the graveside. Deacon Miller had given precise instructions that there would be no visiting hours. He'd permitted a memorial service but told Izzie to have just a few loved ones at the grave to witness the final departure of his earthen vessel.

Following the service, Charlie hugged and kissed my mother and offered condolences to Izzie. He shook Zach's hand, then gave him a hug. As he did the same to me, he whispered, "We've got to talk. Meet me at the old street basketball court around eight, after it gets dark."

I nodded but did not say a word. What he was doing could cost him his job…or maybe his life.

CHAPTER 22

Sabawoon Habibi awoke early in the wilderness near Jalalabad. He left his tent on the mountainside and walked into the crisp air and yellow rays of breaking dawn.

Something bothered him. It could have been a hunch or maybe intuition, but he operated on neither. As the leader of the Taliban in the area, he didn't have time for conjecture. The land was beautiful, but still not free. Although American soldiers had ended their combat mission, enough of them remained behind to impede the progress of both the Taliban and ISIS.

But they would leave. With each death of an American soldier, the resolve of the American government weakened. Yes, they would soon pull out even the last of their armed forces.

He paused at the brink of a cliff to drink in the beauty of the mountain, the sky, and the sun, and thanked Allah for his contact within the White House. Habibi had waited years to avenge the death of his brother, but now everything was in place. Revenge truly tasted sweet. It was why he had chosen Pittsburgh as the target for the sleeper cell. It is why he had entangled Orval Miller with Rev. Amin—why Miller had to die.

Now he had the Army ranger who murdered his brother caught in the web. Black Rose, his agent in Pittsburgh, was well trained. She would eliminate the ranger soon. Habibi would get satisfaction and at the same time strike a damaging blow to America. Soon, he would make his move to gain his glorious place in the caliphate.

Filled with sweetness of revenge, he stalked back to his tent and threw back the flap. He stopped at the sound of his name.

One of his soldiers approached and held out a piece of paper. "A messenger brought this an hour ago. I decoded it and felt you needed to see it as soon as you awoke."

Habibi snatched it from the man's hand. The note was short but not sweet. Complications had arisen in Pittsburgh.

He crumpled the paper and threw it on the ground. It did not matter. The sleeper cell in the city already had its orders. That mission's importance far outweighed this distraction. But he would need to contact a neighboring cell. "Get me the strategists!" Spit flew toward the solider as Habibi barked the order.

Soon after, four bearded men wearing their symbolic black turbans sat across from one another near the warmth of the kerosene heater inside Habibi's tent. They sipped their green tea as they ate traditional Afghan flatbreads.

"Our next target is in Pittsburgh, as you know, but one of our major financiers is close to being compromised. Fortunately, he does not know of our greater jihad in that city.

"A message came from our contact. The assassin's codename is the Black Rose. She faces a greater adversary than she thought, one who trained here in our homeland and took many lives of good jihadists. He is a killer of Muslim men, women, and children. I swore upon my brother's memory that I would avenge his death and see this infidel eliminated. But she was not informed of his capabilities because we believed she could handle him easily."

He said smoothly, calmly, "I cannot assign our sleeper cell in Pittsburgh to pick up the task, as they are already deep in their plans. I cannot compromise their mission. I must contact a proficient soldier to eliminate the problem."

"Is it wise to take this fight, and your personal fight, to the United States, on their soil?" Habibi's elder had obviously been rethinking the plan at hand. "I am not sure we want to rekindle the American war machine now that Afghanistan is ripe for our retaking. With the assistance of ISIS, I believe we can secure a stronghold here once again. Your plan will put us back on the defensive for many years to come."

Habibi smiled. "I have given that much thought. If you remember, we took the jihad to their embassies, blamed the violence on a movie, and they did not retaliate. They will do anything to avoid us. We will begin this jihad by striking a horrible blow that will make the Pittsburgh rivers run red with infidel blood. That is the sign for the sleeper cells to arise; the dawn of the Caliphate will break in the West."

After more discussion, Habibi decided upon an experienced man, Abdul Qadir—code name Nightstalker. A guide for the security forces for several of the Detroit-area mosques, he would eliminate the infidel forces worrying the Black Rose, and do it at any cost, short of compromising the mission.

CHAPTER 23

Rafi loaded his luggage and his package into the Hummer, which idled by the side of the road awaiting its driver for the nighttime trip across the border. It was such a simple thing, smuggling an item through Mexico into the U.S.

He placed the last bag in the Hummer and looked around. Through the dusk he could see the driver leaning against a dilapidated building not far away, smoking a cigarette.

Rafi shoved the door closed as his secure satellite phone rang. He stared at the phone for a moment before answering. Sabawoon Habibi, the gifted leader he'd waited for for so long, would not risk a direct call to him except for a very serious matter.

"Yes, Sabawoon," Rafi answered.

"Is everything in place?" Habibi asked.

"Loading the vehicle now. I should be in Pittsburgh in plenty of time. Everything is back on track." After a brief pause, Rafi chose to question his leader. "Is there is a problem?"

"There are some loose ends in Pittsburgh with our financier. I am taking care of those now, before this boil becomes a festering wound. I had to go to our friends in Detroit to bring in a holy warrior to replace the Black Rose, who has failed us."

Rafi frowned. Failure was not acceptable.

Habibi continued. "Our financier Amin's actions have placed some of our future plans in jeopardy. We will be severing our ties with him during your strike. Keep a low profile until the day of reckoning."

Rafi nodded into the phone. "We will take extra precautions. Do I know our friend from Detroit?"

"Nothing for you to worry about. Amin created a mess, and now I need a janitor to clean it up. Our Detroit friend should take care of it quickly. If there is anything that might endanger the cell, I will let you know. What have you heard from our friend in Washington?"

"She obtained all of the target's travel plans, time of arrival at the school and the details of the day, and sent them to me."

The greatest attack was only days away and the CIA, FBI and Homeland Security had no idea that they were compromised by one woman's deception. The Americans were so easy to predict and deceive. Their freedom was the rope Rafi would hang them with.

"Good. Rafi. I've decided to ask you not to martyr yourself in this attack. We feel that you are the one to lead our greater battle to follow. Will you be my general in the battle to take down the United States?"

Rafi frowned. "I am ready to see paradise, Sabawoon. That is my dream, my destiny."

"Spoken like a true mujahideen. I promise that you will see paradise, but it will be in our next attack. I am only asking that you delay your arrival with the seventy-two virgins until that time. You are my best soldier, and I need you there."

Slowly Rafi scuffed a shoe on the gravel pavement and sighed. "Yes, Sabawoon, I will delay my martyrdom for the greater jihad."

"Good. I will update you once the mess in Pittsburgh is cleaned up. It won't take long."

Habibi, seated in the chilly morning air in his tent, hung up the phone.

He took a deep breath and punched numbers for another call.

Holy warriors needed to unite. And even he could see that the united banners would not be under the Taliban, which was losing foreign recruits to the Islamic State.

He too would swear his allegiance to the caliph of the Islamic State. His strike on the Great Satan would assure him a position of great importance in the new organization.

CHAPTER 24

After Orval's graveside service, I ate lunch with Izzie and my family and dropped off my mother at the Baptist Senior Home. I also sneaked in and dropped off my would-be assassin's gun at the forensics lab for testing before returning to my apartment.

I glanced at my watch. I had hours to kill before meeting with Charlie at eight o'clock. Too keyed up to sit, I decided to tackle the heap of Post Gazettes that buried my kitchen table. Maybe it would be a good distraction. I flipped to the sports page of the paper on top. Once I read everything about the Steelers and the NBA, I went to the front page.

Few of the articles interested me, but one made me laugh. A local crack house had been raided by a man who claimed to be a cop. The intruder told them God's vengeance was upon them. The police commented that they had no leads or suspects at this time. They nicknamed the impostor cop 'Dirty Harry.' I liked that. Plus, there was no mention of Mandy.

The article next to it drew my attention. I took a seat and folded the paper before reading it. A local Pittsburgh-area elementary school had been selected for a trial of the latest version of the lunch program initiative made popular, or unpopular according to the kids, by the first lady. The article stated that the first lady would visit the school in a few days to publicize her pet project. The program had made what was termed "more palatable adjustments" to school lunch menus.

It made a lot of sense to do the launch in Pittsburgh as the blue-collar city transitioned to white-collar tech jobs. The conservative communities meant to let no one write the project off as a liberal invasion of civil rights or perceive the area as a haven for West Coast nutcases. Pittsburgh was Pittsburgh, and that meant mainstream.

I skimmed article after article, but not much else caught my attention. By the time I'd sifted through most of the pile, it was time to leave. What magazines remained, I tossed in the recycling bin. News that far down in the heap was old anyway.

As I drove to the meeting, I wondered what was up with Charlie. The old basketball court was out-of-the-way, in an unlit area, and rarely used at night except for gang parties.

I turned off my lights a block away and rounded the corner. Suspicion and paranoia were running my every move by this time.

I heard the familiar thump of a basketball being dribbled. Charlie was already there, so I jogged to the court. "You brought me all the way out here for a game of one-on-one?"

"Just thought I would have a better cover story with this ball in my hands." He shot the ball toward the hoop, but it bounced off the rim. Instead of chasing the rebound, though, he looked straight at me. "You know this is going to cost me my job, my family's security, and most likely my reputation. Lamb doesn't play fair."

"I know all that, which is why I know what you have to say is important enough for you to risk everything." I chased the ball down, then shot it back to Charlie. I needed to do all I could to protect him, but Lamb would get his licks in first. "So what do you have for me?"

"First of all, Lamb's secretary, Anna Maria, blew her stack in his office after the memorial service. Her hand had swollen to twice its size, and she was cursing you. She called you an infidel, by the way."

I laughed at that. A telling choice of words.

"Most importantly, I went to see Lorenzo yesterday at the jail. He had a written note he snuck to me. I didn't want to ask where he kept it, but it's for Izzie," Charlie said in a quiet tone, as he handed me a small, tightly rolled piece of paper.

"Did you read it?"

"Yeah, I didn't know who it was for until I read it. Basically, he's telling Izzie that her dad gave him something to hide. Also, if anything ever happened to him, he was to give whatever he was hiding to Izzie. He didn't speak about it. All I know is what's in the note."

I unrolled the note. It was short but packed a punch.

Deacon gave me something to hide for Izzie. He said she would defend me.

"You better get out of here before anyone sees you talking to me, Charlie."

"It's too late. I saw Anna Maria's red Mustang go by a few minutes before you came around the corner. I already know how they are going to come after me. Since I work with kids, it's too easy to set up for them to do anything else. I will be accused of molesting a youth group member. They already have the girl primed. I saw her whispering to her friends last Sunday, and when I walked by, they all gave me icy stares. I didn't know what it meant until one of the other kids got a text from her by mistake and showed me."

He ran toward the basketball hoop, took a mighty leap, and stuffed the ball into the hoop with both hands—a perfectly executed dunk. After he grabbed the ball again, he stopped in front of me. "You know I'm innocent, but one accusation like that will put my ministry on ice. I know I can't fight it; I just want a little justice. And I'll need to talk to Izzie about defending me as well." His eyes filled with tears.

I placed my hands on his shoulders and looked him in the eyes. "I'll ask her. And I promise I'll dig up the truth so you're exonerated. We'll beat this thing." I wrapped my arms around him, but at the crack of a gunshot, the hug became a tackle, and I pulled Charlie to the ground with me.

CHAPTER 25

I looked in the direction of the gunshot to see four thugs strutting our way. Their guns were tilted to the side in a violent attempt to look cool. It wasn't the way anyone with an ounce of training held a gun, but either way their weapons were lethal.

"Stay down!" I told Charlie as I rolled away. I pulled one gun from my waistband and the other from the holster at my shoulder, then leaped to my feet.

Four gun barrels stared at me. The thugs grinned behind them. Their faces said my chances were slim and I was about to meet my maker.

Two muzzles flashed at the other end of the park, followed by two blasts. Bullets kicked up gravel between the legs of the four gang bangers, spraying dirt and gravel against their designer jeans. Suddenly, they didn't like the odds and scattered.

I aimed both of my guns toward the figure walking out of the dark. He put his hands in the air and called out, "I'm a friendly, Jude."

I knew the voice, but it had been years since I heard it last. Could it really be my old friend? "Identify yourself."

"Have I been gone that long? You are right, though; I should identify myself. This is Jack Hesidence, with the U.S. government. Request permission to approach." Hesidence's laughter filled the air and broke the tension.

I pulled Charlie to his feet and introduced him to Hesidence.

Hesidence shook my hand with a firm grip.

I had to know. "Why are you here, Hesidence? I'm not complaining, because you saved our bacon just now, but it would still be good to know."

"In town to do some work. I was driving the old neighborhood and saw my old car. I never should have sold it to you and figured you couldn't be too far away from it. I was coming on the park when I heard the shots. I just reacted," he said.

"Charlie, go home and trust that Izzie and I will get you out of this mess. We will be there at your arraignment," I said.

Charlie gave Hesidence a once-over and must have decided to trust him. He scooped up his basketball, said goodnight, and walked to his car. Once he was on his way home, Hesidence and I continued our discussion.

"I heard you became a spook," I said.

"Almost to the top of the food chain," Hesidence said with a smile.

"Then why are you here and not behind a desk?" Odd that he should rise so far when his view on radical jihadists differed so much from the new president's. The president of the U.S., POTUS, believed terrorism could be beat with diplomacy and the correction of past grievous errors made by his predecessors. Hesidence just believed in rousting terrorist cells with whatever force was necessary.

"Really can't say, but you can trust that I'm not far away from you at any given time. I've already been briefed by your old partner, Ed Rivers. I know the general details, but if I trained you right, your gut has taken you a lot further. What do you have?" Hesidence pulled his coat tighter and flipped up the collar.

"Would you like to get some coffee and talk?" I asked when I noticed his shiver.

He shook his head. "Love to, but duty calls. I have a few other details to check on."

"It's about a murder. Nothing on a National Security level. That's about it."

"Tomorrow for that coffee, and I do want to know everything you know." His cell phone rang. He held up a finger, telling me to wait. "Hesidence here. When did he leave? Do we have an ETA? I'll have assets on his tail when he arrives." He pocketed the phone. "Gotta run, Jude. Coffee at four tomorrow afternoon at Tom's."

I shook my head as I watched Hesidence disappear into the darkness. I supposed he spent most of his time gathering intelligence inside Iraq. So what was he doing here in Pittsburgh? And how did it relate to my case? Once I left the park, I raced to tell Izzie that I had two new clients for her fledgling law firm.

When Izzie opened the door, she wore a surprised expression. "You're back so early." She grabbed my hands and pulled me into the apartment as she peppered me with rapid-fire questions. "Did Charlie give you some information about Dad's killer? What do you have?" I wanted to tell her that she was sounding like a cop but thought better of it.

"Charlie said your dad gave whatever it is to Lorenzo Deets. He has it hidden."

"How do we get to him?"

"The only way to get to him is to do what your father told him you would do."

Her face scrunched into a look of total perplexity.

"Your dad told Lorenzo that if anything happened to him you would defend him. The arraignment is tomorrow morning, by the way."

"If Dad wanted me to represent him, then he had his reasons. I'll do it." But her tone held questions, as though she wasn't sure that taking the case would give us the answers we needed. But no one ever questioned what Orval Miller said we should do.

"There's one more thing." I filled her in on the events of the night in broad terms, including Lamb's plan to wrongly accuse Charlie. Her hand flew to her mouth in shock.

"I guess I'm back in the courtroom." She sat up straighter and her words rang with determination. "Can you help me with the cases? I'll need a good gumshoe for both, and there isn't any better than Jude Cameron," she said with an irresistible smile.

Suddenly she jumped from the couch. "Oh, I almost forgot. I found something behind that Proverbs verse picture frame. Dad left a note, but it seems like nonsense to me." She dashed into the kitchen and returned with a folded sheet of paper. "Can you figure it out?" She handed it to me and stood close as we stared at the paper.

I read it twice. Complete gibberish! It read, "!$@b3((@."

I shook my head. "I'm not getting any psychic vibe. I'll have Mom ask King Solomon for some help." When I realized I'd come to trust this person I'd never met, I laughed. "Here I am asking a dementia patient to ask a man who thinks he is a Biblical king to translate something in gibberish."

This time we both laughed. She still stood close — a lot closer than recent times had permitted. Izzie wasn't backing off, and I felt like I needed to kiss her. I wanted to kiss her. But I could have been getting all my signals crossed. Why was this love stuff so hard? Another question for King Solomon.

CHAPTER 26

At eight a.m. I walked into the courtyard of the courthouse. The grand fountain had been shut off for the winter, but the elegant design still impressed me.

Izzie arrived moments behind me. "We're in luck. Joe O'Donnell is the judge assigned to Lorenzo's case." I grinned as we walked down the amazing hallway. The richness of the magnificent, artistic beauty thrilled me, as always, but today it was overshadowed by this turn of good luck.

We arrived at Judge Joe O'Donnell's chambers and knocked. Izzie had filed to replace the public defender with herself, but she wanted to make sure he knew she was Deets's defense attorney, and that she needed to meet with him before the arraignment. Izzie was looking for a favor from her father's old friend.

O'Donnell's secretary asked them to wait while she went in to talk to the judge. Moments later, he busted out of his office. "Isabella Miller, it is so good to see you. Give me a big hug."

They hugged and he took her face in his hands gently while staring straight into her eyes. "Isabella, I have no idea why you are defending the accused killer of your father, but this sounds like something Orval would have done."

O'Donnell pointed at her and looked at me before saying, "This apple didn't fall too far from the tree. She's just like her old man." As O'Donnell turned toward his chamber' door he called out to his secretary to give us any access we needed.

After the brief meeting, Judge O'Donnell, Izzie and I were guided to a small room where we could speak with Lorenzo "privately," but we knew hidden microphones and cameras would record the meeting.

Moments later, the door opened, and Lorenzo entered. The two guards who had brought him took up spots outside, on either side of the door.

Izzie smiled at Deets and shook his hand. "Hello, Lorenzo. I'm Isabella Miller, your defense attorney."

Deets broke into a smile that almost ate his ears.

Since Izzie didn't want him to say a word, she quickly handed him a legal notepad. Written on the top page were the words, We are bugged and videotaped, so say nothing and keep a straight face. Just write yes or no on the paper. Then she asked him a series of yes-or-no questions.

He followed instructions well. In a few minutes they were done.

"If you think of anything more I must know," Izzie wrote to Deets, "please tell me in the courtroom. Simply whisper in my ear."

I rapped twice on the door to alert the guards, and one opened the door for us. Outside, Izzie pointed down the hallway. "That went well. Now, let's go see Charlie. From the call I got from a friend of mine at the jail, the prosecutor rushed this case through in the early hours of the morning. It smells of another set-up, but I do not have any details beyond that. My guess is that the evidence has been cooked."

He was being held down the hall. As we opened the door to his holding room, I stopped and stared. Behind me, Izzie let out a quiet gasp. Charlie tried to smile, but all that did was show several missing teeth. Bruises colored his face purple and blue, punctuated by swollen, black eyes and a fat lip. And the way he held his side made me suspect he had some broken ribs as well.

"What happened, Charlie?"

"Those four guys from the park were waiting for me at my house with a dozen other men. One of them claimed to be my accuser's father. I found out later that they had already gotten to Robin and beaten her. Thankfully, she was able to get the kids to hide upstairs before they broke in.

"When the cops got there, they took a long time dispersing the crowd. I asked them to check on my wife and call for an ambulance. Instead, they cuffed me, tossed me in the back of their car, and brought me here." He swiped at the blood oozing from his split lip. "Please, Jude. I need to know how Robin and the kids are." Tears clouded his eyes and thickened his voice.

"I'll find out and get you the news after the arraignment," I assured him.

Izzie stepped in. "I don't expect there will be a high bail for this charge. We should have you free this afternoon."

"You don't know, then." Sorrow filled his eyes. "Lamb decided to get real dirty. Tyffani was strangled to death with the socks I keep in my gym bag at my church office. I'm up the proverbial creek without a paddle." He dropped his head into his hands and sobbed.

My heart broke for him. The Dirty Harry side of me added a few more names to the list of people who would receive a 'come to Jesus' visit.

Izzie touched my elbow. "Jude, we have to find out when she was murdered. We know where he was at eight p.m. We just need to establish his alibi from the time of the memorial service until he met you. That should clear his name."

"Iz, we're not dealing with first-timer, stupid criminals. The people behind this kind of frame get away with murder all the time. I'm sure any alibi he might have has left Pittsburgh for an extended vacation." I smacked my hand on the wall in frustration.

An hour later, Izzie and I sat, barely speaking as we waited for Lorenzo's hearing to begin. Inside I was seething. My fists clenched and unclenched in a rapid, angry movement. Izzie stared off into space, but I knew she was analyzing her next several legal moves.

Once inside the courtroom, Lorenzo was led in and pushed into the chair next to Izzie. I sat close behind them. As the judge entered, the boy whispered to her.

Izzie's mouth dropped open. She whispered back, and he responded.

Then he sat back to listen to the prosecutor.

Izzie scratched out a note and passed it to me.

I read it while rubbing my chin. Orval had given Deets a thumb drive that was to go to her. The boy had hidden it inside an old model airplane on the shelf in his bedroom. He didn't know what was on it.

I would be picking that up later, for certain.

CHAPTER 27

As soon as both arraignments were finished, I bolted to the Chevelle and roared over to Charlie's house. The place was empty—it had been trashed. A neighbor stopped in to tell me they had taken Robin to Allegheny General, and the kids were with their grandmother.

"What happened?" I asked as we walked to the front lawn.

The middle-aged woman stifled a sob with one hand. "After the police took Charlie away, the mob broke in. All the neighbors called 911 over and over, but no one came to help." She took a deep breath. "We heard screams for a long time. Then they brought Robin outside and dumped her on the lawn. I don't want to think about, let alone say, what they did to her.

"My husband grabbed his shotgun and went out to stop it. They laughed at him and threw bottles. One hit him on the head, and he's had a headache ever since." She shook her head. "Who would do such a thing?"

I had my suspicions as to who was behind it, and maybe a messenger, a cruel messenger, would have to visit him.

I thanked the woman and started to walk back to my car but stopped when a large black Suburban rolled up behind it.

The rear door opened, and Hesidence stepped out. "I just came from the hospital. Charlie's wife will heal physically, but I'm not sure about mentally and emotionally."

I clenched my fists.

He said gravely, "Last night we caught some chatter on social media that led us to this address. The idiots posted videos of what they did to Charlie's wife on YouTube. They beat her so bad that she was begging for them to put her out of her misery. We broke it up and got her to the hospital."

My pulse quickened. How could it have gotten so out of hand?

Hesidence was shaking his head. "We have a couple of the perps in custody, and the rest will be arrested and detained in the next several days. The whole bunch will see some well-deserved jail time for this. I hope that rogue cop, the guy the newspapers called Dirty Harry, doesn't visit them. You don't know anything about that, do you, Jude? He did quite a job on a crack house over on Bluff Street. Payback should come in court."

I didn't flinch, just stared at him, my blood coming to a slow boil.

"We also got the kids to Gramma's where they will be safe," Hesidence said, as he let out a deep sigh of frustration. "The two of them stayed hidden and locked in their rooms. Both of them are traumatized but not physically harmed. I have a car on that house, and one on your brother's every move."

"Thanks, Hesidence, for doing all that, but isn't this a little out of your jurisdiction?" And how'd he know about my brother's problems?

"Being a good guy is never out of my jurisdiction," Hesidence said as he lifted his chin and sucked in another breath. But he quickly dropped the pose and his expression sobered. "I need to ask you to go into protective custody. You know way too much, and someone wants you dead. According to an intercepted transmission, they've called in a professional assassin from Detroit just to deal with you. You did something to tick off someone very powerful."

I shook my head. "Hesidence, I've been racking my brain to

come up with a reason why I seem to be a special target. I just assumed it is because I didn't fold on the Deets case. But maybe there's something more. Could Deacon Miller's death be that tied into whatever you are working on?" I ran both my hands through my buzz-cut hair. I was trying to massage the answer to the surface, but no theories stuck out.

From Hesidence's stone-faced expression, I got the feeling he was holding back information.

He turned to the side and frowned. "Unfortunately, there is more to all this that I can't talk about. We're tailing the assassin, but he is good enough that he'll lose us at some time and make a move on you. He won't miss, and he won't go down with a simple thrown elbow."

Protective custody wasn't my style. "You know I can't." I shook my head hard and turned to my car. Protective custody wouldn't solve the Deacon's murder or protect those I loved.

He laughed and shrugged in resignation. "I'm still expecting us to meet at four at Tom's. Stay alive and bring me everything you have." He climbed back in his car. He was still shaking his head as the Suburban drove away.

Charlie and Robin's attackers would have to wait to hear from me, but I planned on getting a little street justice against any of them that might be set free. I planned to deliver a message that the streets belonged to me. If the perps refused to listen, then my message would have to be cruel.

CHAPTER 28

I decided to pick up the thumb drive at LoDee's house. Izzie had talked to his mother after the arraignment and set up a plan for me to pick up the device on which our entire investigation hinged.

I gave Mrs. Deets a hug to console her, then sat down on an old couch. My body sank into the lifeless pillows. "I believe there is some hope for Lorenzo, Mrs. Deets. I can't talk about it now, but I believe that what he has in his room will work to free him." I spoke in a calming and reassuring tone.

The middle-aged woman's face lit up for the first time. "He isn't a bad boy. Deacon Miller changed his life or should I say, the Lord Jesus changed his life, but you're a preacher's kid, so you know all about how faith can change people. Your daddy was my pastor. It must have given you a tremendous foundation for your faith just living with him." She rattled on like we were going to break out in a revival.

I gave her my best fake smile. She had no idea that my faith foundation had so many cracks and holes, and I wasn't about to confess my doubts to a woman who needed to hear nothing but hope. I took her hand in mine and squeezed it.

After a moment of silence, I got off the couch and went in Lorenzo's bedroom, pulled down the airplane, and snatched the thumb drive.

I hid it in the lining of my coat, thanked Mrs. Deets for her cooperation, and walked out.

Seeing Mrs. Deets reminded me that I hadn't seen Mom yet today, and it was time to stop by the Baptist Senior Home. She should be getting close to lunch and wouldn't want to keep me too long. A good thing, because I had a lot to do.

I waved to the nurses as I passed their station, but I didn't have to go all the way to Mom's room. As soon as I turned the corner, I saw the bright, neon green sweatshirt with the green bouquet of flowers embroidered across her chest, the one she insisted on wearing when she exercised. It nearly blinded me as she hobbled down the hall with her walker to steady her.

"Looking good, Mom. How many laps are you doing today?"

She just scoffed at my attempt at humor. "There is nothing to laugh at, Jude. Even at my age, you have to exercise."

"I was just trying to offer encouragement. Why the sudden interest in getting your exercise?"

"There's a big party tonight, and I'm sure King Solomon is going to ask me to dance. I thought I'd try out some of my moves before we cut a rug."

"What does 'cut a rug' mean?" Dad would often turn on the radio, snatch her small frame in his big arms and say, "Let's cut a rug." But I never understood the phrase.

"Dance! It means to dance, my young son. It means to have a good time, which is something you have forgotten how to do." Mom wagged her finger.

I gave her a convincing smile. "As soon as I catch Orval Miller's killer, I'll take a long vacation to some nice beach."

"You'll have to go alone, because I sure can't go with you." Her face scrunched into a scowl.

"I'm sure someone will go with me on a vacation."

"That nice young girl you were with yesterday looked at you as if she would go on a vacation with you anywhere. What was her name again?"

116

"That is Orval Miller's daughter, Isabella."

"That skinny, little, knock-kneed girl from my Sunday school class? My goodness, Jude, she turned into a real tomato. You better grab onto that one before someone else does. Remember what your dad said: 'Always listen to your mother.'"

Her shoulders rounded, and she gripped the walker in front of her. "I'm tired now, Jude. Please help me back to my bed."

With my hand on her back as she shuffled toward her room, we slowly made our way down the hallway. She sat down on her bed and let out a long sigh of relief. She glanced at the Bible next to her with a puzzled look. It was her look when she had forgotten something important.

"Mom, is there a verse you want me to read? Did King Solomon give you a verse to pass on to me?"

She brightened. "Yes, he did. Jude. Tell the nurse that I'll have dinner later. I need a nap right now." I lifted her legs up onto the bed. As her eyes closed she said in a quiet voice, "Proverbs 28:17." Only moments later, she snored peacefully.

She would need her rest for the night's activities. "That King Solomon must be quite a live wire," I whispered softly over her sleeping body.

Once I was in my car I opened the Bible to Proverbs 28:17. It said, "A man that doeth violence to the blood of any person shall flee to the pit; let no man stay him." Well, that one really helped. There were dozens of men involved in this case who had done bloody violence. And what was this pit thing? I'd tell Izzie later, and maybe she could decipher the meaning.

CHAPTER 29

I arrived at Tom's Diner early to find the usually crowded diner sparsely populated. Maybe it had something to do with the piece of plywood covering the shattered window.

I sat a few booths down so I could watch for the large, black Suburban. I was still in the middle of trying to figure out why government spooks all drove those enormous vehicles when Hesidence strolled up and slid into the seat across from me.

"I take it the broken window is from your last visit?" Hesidence joked.

"My little friend in the red Mustang decided she would show me how angry she was. I got my payback, though."

Hesidence laughed into the coffee I had ordered for him. "She failed her assignment. I suppose we'll find her floating in some river in another part of the world."

"That means I am no longer in danger, right?" But I knew the answer to my question would be a negative.

"She has been replaced. We followed your new assassin from Detroit. He is nicknamed the Nightstalker. You won't see him, but he'll be there. He doesn't know we're there as well." After another sip of coffee, he shifted gears. "That's all I can tell you, but I need everything you know, no matter how trivial."

I laid everything out for him, step by step, from the day Mom told me about her visit from Orval Miller through the last Proverb only an hour ago.

Hesidence nodded every once in a while, but asked no questions and took no notes. Strange. I didn't recall his memory being that good.

I studied him for a moment, then asked, "Do you have a photographic memory now?"

"No, I'm always wired. Every word you say is not only recorded but also run through a cross-referencing data bank. Okay, now I know what you know, but I still have some questions. How is Amin tied to you?"

"Izzie's dad was an old friend of mine, and from what Izzie said, Amin bought into her dad's business when it was going under. Of course, the mayor manufactured that crisis. Money is at the root of their evil. There is no doubt in my mind." I pounded my fist on the table. "Amin, the mayor and Lamb are all tied to the money trail. I don't know where the money comes from, but I think Orval uncovered it."

Hesidence nodded slowly, as if he was fitting this piece into the puzzle of this case. "Let me give you some facts, and you can draw some conclusions. A large amount of heroin was dumped in our country recently. Each time a dealer got his portion, he cut it to heighten his profits. Because of that, we simply tested the drugs we confiscated for purity and found Ground Zero, which is Pittsburgh."

I didn't have to consider it. "My conclusion is that Amin is bringing it into this country, but I don't know how or from where."

"Think about what you know of Amin, and you'll figure this out. When you do, it will lead you to more pieces of the puzzle. I want you to bring me those pieces." He stopped talking, smiled for a second time, and began again. "First thing we do, though, is visit Izzie and unlock the info on that thumb drive. No doubt it will help convict Amin. But I want her there when we open it." He glanced at his watch. "Call her and let her know we will pick her up in fifteen minutes."

When we arrived, Izzie waited by the front door to her building. One of Hesidence's men stepped out of the Suburban and opened the door, and she climbed into the back seat with us. The vehicle started driving slowly around the neighborhood.

Her eyes widened when she looked at Hesidence. "You look a lot like Jack Hesidence, who used to live around here."

He grinned at her. "It is me, Izzie. I didn't think it had been that long since I left. It's good to see you, and I am sorry for your loss. Your dad was a good friend to everyone."

Izzie bit her lip, but managed to hold back the tears threatening in the corners of her eyes. She reached out her hand, and Hesidence took it. He slid to the edge of his seat and held her hand until Izzie composed herself.

Meanwhile, some strong feelings came out of nowhere for me. I should be the one holding her hand, not Hesidence.

He held up the thumb drive I'd given to him on the way to pick up Izzie. "Jude recovered the thumb drive from your client's home. I thought you'd like to be here when we took a look at it."

"Thank you," she mumbled.

I looked around the large vehicle. It was loaded with technology I had never seen before. It was certainly nothing that an average street detective would have in one of his police force vehicles.

The technician in the Suburban's third row seat flipped his laptop open and tapped the keyboard. When he held out his hand, Hesidence placed the thumb drive on his open palm. He stuck it into the side of the computer and clicked a few more keys. "The information is password protected. Does anyone know the password?" He stared at Izzie.

Izzie rattled off possibilities, and the technician typed them in one after the other. Each time, he shook his head. None worked.

Hesidence held up a hand. "If your dad went to all this trouble to leave you this information and it's password–protected, then he surely chose a password you would be able to figure out, Izzie. Think for a minute."

"I got it." A flare of light danced in her eyes. "It's my name."

"We tried your name, ma'am," said the technician.

"Yeah, but not this way." She opened a pocket on the side of her purse and pulled out a scrap of paper. "We found this behind a frame on a picture in Dad's Sunday school classroom. These symbols look like the letters that spell my name." She handed him the scrap of paper with !$@b3((@ written on it. The tech typed it in.

He shook his head with a sheepish grin. "Why didn't I think of that? We're in. It looks like financial records showing large sums of money moved to off-shore accounts. I can find out who the accounts belong to with a few hours' time."

After a few more clicks, he said, "Next is a series of emails from a Rev. Amin to a foreign contact. By the data accompanying the messages, it appears to be something to do with Afghanistan. Given time I can trace the responses back and give us a better idea who it is." He practically rubbed his hands together. Clearly he thrived on this stuff.

Hesidence leaned over the seat to look at the screen in front of the technician. "These are explosive. This is why Miller was assassinated. They found out he had these documents."

"It gives dates." The technician scrolled through one of the messages and pointed to the screen. "It appears the big shipment came in about three months ago on the eighteenth."

"We could see where Amin was on that day and tie him to it," Hesidence said.

Izzie spoke up. "I can tell you where he was. Nineteen young people from his mission were killed by a suicide bomber in Afghanistan. On the eighteenth, he conducted memorials for them. I attended them all. He'll have alibis up to his ears."

"Jude, didn't you uncover something about students with Amin's organization, Co-exist, who were killed on a trip to Afghanistan?" Hesidence asked as he leaned back into his seat.

I nodded as the pieces began to fall into place. "I assumed it was drug-related. Now I'm beginning to see that my hunch was right. But what doesn't make sense is why he didn't pick up and leave town like he did in Cleveland. What's holding him here?"

"More money to be made," Hesidence scoffed.

"He has another group of students ready to go to Afghanistan," Izzie added. "He probably has a memorial service already penciled in on his schedule."

Hesidence scratched his head. "There's more to it, but I haven't figured it out. I'll research these documents and be in touch, but, Jude, be careful. This Nightstalker that's been sent after you is a serious killer. We'll be a step behind him, but you need to stay two steps ahead if you plan on staying alive."

The vehicle drew to a stop in front of Izzie's building, and she climbed out. Once she'd entered the building, the large SUV pulled away.

The Suburban took me back to my car at Tom's Diner. I got in and headed for home. If Hesidence spoke with the police about Charlie and pushed for jailing Robin's attackers, that would certainly raise the ire of B. A. Lamb. I would have to be extra careful when I visited him in the morning. He wouldn't be feeling pastoral, and who knew how he would take out his anger?

CHAPTER 30

When I pulled into the First Baptist Church parking lot, it was close to eight a.m. The good Reverend B. A. Lamb's Lexus sat alone in the parking lot. I had timed it perfectly, since I wanted some up-close and private time with the good Reverend.

My footsteps made a familiar sound as I walked down the hall to what used to be my father's office. A light shone from the crack under the door. I pushed it open without knocking.

"What the—" Lamb looked up with genuine fear in his eyes as I walked quickly to his desk. He gasped as I grabbed his expensive silk tie with a hard yank.

Lamb came sliding across the top of his desk. His bulk pushed papers, pens and books to the floor with crashing thuds.

I placed my gun on the desk in front of him. With my best Dirty Harry impersonation—something I couldn't resist—I said, "Go ahead; make my day."

Fear shone in his eyes, and his body quivered. "You can't do this," he choked out. "I will report you. I'll sue you and...."

His voice trailed off as I picked up my gun, aimed it at him, and cocked it.

"My good reverend, I've been reading the Bible a lot lately. I came across a verse in Proverbs. You might recall it. 'A soft answer turneth away wrath: but grievous words stir up anger.'

"I thought we could play the Proverbs 15:1 game. It's simple. I ask a question and a true, soft answer will turn away my wrath.

123

On the other hand, words that grieve my soul will surely stir up my anger. Do we have an understanding?" I asked in a slow, deeply serious tone.

"I won't answer a thing. I am a man of the cloth, and you will surely rot in hell for this. I curse you." Lamb seethed.

"Grievous words." I pulled tight enough on his necktie that the knot at his neck choked off his air supply. "Maybe you didn't understand, Reverend Lamb. Let's try again. Do you understand?"

"You miserable piece of —"

I cut off whatever crass word he'd planned to call me with another tug on his tie. His fat little legs kicked behind him like a hanging man dancing. I hoped he responded soon because my anger was subsiding and the better man was starting to win out inside my soul. Lamb finally nodded, and I eased back on the knot but retained my controlling grip.

"Who set up Charlie, and who killed the girl?"

"If I answer, she'll kill me."

My eyes registered my shock at his answer, but I had recent news for Lamb. "I suspect she may already be dead, but there is another killer. This time, he's hunting the both of us. So answer the question, and I can get you some protection." These were some true and some not-so-true things. The Nightstalker might be after me, but I couldn't guarantee he wasn't sent to kill Lamb too. Nor could I protect him from it. The truth was that I was a ship floating in a dark sea with no anchor and no mooring.

"Set me free and I'll tell you what you want to know. I want a deal, though. I want immunity," he said as I allowed my grip to relax. He slid back to his side of the desk into his plush chair as he massaged his neck.

"I can get the immunity for you," I said, knowing he would not likely live long enough to enjoy it. "But before I call the feds, you have to give me enough to show them it's worth it. What about Orval Miller? Why was he killed?"

"I don't know, and Amin says he doesn't either. He was as shocked as I was. That decision came from somewhere else. I knew we were next if we screwed up." Sweat poured off his forehead. "You need to get me protection. Now. And I'll testify if I have immunity. I don't want to go to jail. I just want to start over somewhere else. I can change. I promise." His eyes pleaded with me.

A rifle shot cut his plea short. The bullet broke the stained glass window in his office with a crack and a crash of glass. It splintered the bookcase behind him.

My Dirty Harry attitude dissipated, and the good cop pushed forward. I dove across the desk like Troy Polamalu, a Steelers linebacker known for impressive jumping. We crashed to the floor.

At the shriek of tires burning rubber, I rolled off of Lamb, but I knew it was already too late to catch sight of the car.

"My advice is to watch yourself, Lamb. It seems you're already on the list to be eliminated." I stood to my feet and walked to the door.

"What about my protection?" he cried out in near tears.

"'For all they that take the sword shall perish with the sword,'" I quoted. "In plain English, you made your bed, now sleep in it."

His curses followed me out the door. I smiled as I patted my pocket, but waited until I reached my car before pulling out the digital recorder. I listened to bits and pieces of our conversation to make sure it had recorded everything. I checked the car for bombs, then took a deep breath, turned the key in the ignition, and drove to the Baptist Senior Home. I needed some normalcy in my life. Yeah, it was pretty bad when I considered Mom a bit of normalcy—even on her good days.

In another couple minutes I sank my exhilarated body into

my familiar visitor's chair.

"What has you smiling so big?"

"I just had a man-to-man talk with Reverend Lamb."

"Wonderful! Did you pummel him a few times for me?"

"Mother, I would never do a thing like that. You raised me to respect my elders." Fake indignation colored my answer.

"No, I taught you to do what is right, and pummeling that sanctimonious son of a...."

I held up a hand to stop her from finishing the phrase. I'd been through a lot lately, but I didn't think I could handle hearing profanity from my saintly mother. "Okay. Yes, I pummeled him one for you." Verbally.

"That's a good boy. What did he say?"

"He cursed me a lot, that's for sure."

"You may not remember your Bible stories as well as I do, but he is mentioned in the Old Testament," she said while sipping her Ensure.

"Reverend Lamb is in the Bible?" She'd slipped to a new low if she couldn't remember her Bible stories anymore.

Mom stared at the bottle sitting on her bedside table. "Did I ever tell you that whenever I want one of these, I just knock on the restaurant's door and say 'Yoo-hoo,'?"

"Can't say you ever did, Mom. What about the Old Testament and Reverend Lamb?" I was eager for a Bible lesson—even a mixed up one, as long as she got around to telling me King Solomon's latest message.

"I almost forgot, but King Solomon reminded me of the talking donkey, although he called it by another word, one more appropriate for Reverend Lamb. King Solomon said that Balaam was a prophet who sold his ability to prophesy a curse on the enemy. In other words, he took his God-given gift and used it to make ill-gotten gain. It wasn't until his donkey spoke to him that he realized his sin and error."

I listened, ashamed that I didn't know the story.

"King Solomon pointed out that even Lamb's name predicted what he is: B. A. Lamb spells 'Balaam' in my Bible dictionary."

"You're right, Mom. King Solomon is a wise man and Lamb is a false prophet. It looks like I was used as the donkey that spoke to him. His heart softened and now he is willing to testify to all his wrongdoings." Noticing Mom's eyes closing slowly I pushed to get any message Solomon had intended for me. "What else did Solomon say? Did he have a verse for me?"

"Are you using these in your daily devotions, Jude?"

"I guess, kind of, yes." I turned my head so she couldn't look me in the eyes.

"Good. Your dad would be proud. Let me see if I can remember that verse he gave me." Mom began to relax in her bed. She suddenly sat upright like something jabbed her in the back. "Did I tell you about the dance?"

"I was going to ask, but we got sidetracked." This time, I answered honestly; I did want to know. Hearing her story was like driving by an accident. You didn't want to know or see, but there was an inner compulsion that drove you to look.

"Well, your old mother got funky. We did the jive from the 1940s and the twist from the sixties. It was a blast, and that sweet, nice King Solomon was a true gentleman all night." Mom leaned close to me and whispered, "He tried to kiss me goodnight." Then she giggled like a school girl with her hands slapped across her laughing mouth.

I grinned. She needed to be happy again. So did I, but that would have to wait.

Suddenly she stopped, puzzlement written over her wrinkles. "What were we talking about? I get so forgetful now. Oh, I remember, that verse from Proverbs. Let me think. Yes, yes, it was Proverbs 19:12."

"Thanks, Mom. I'm really glad you had a good time last

night." I leaned over and kissed her.

"Don't take any wooden nickels," she said, and then laughed out loud. "That's what King Solomon said after he kissed me good night." Her eyes grew wide. "Oh my, I let the cat out of the bag." She slapped both hands over her mouth again, and I could hear her giggling through her fingers as I walked out the door.

A chime from my phone interrupted my thoughts. Before I could pull my phone out, another chime sounded. Two text messages at once, one from Ed Rivers and one from Jack Hesidence. They both said the same thing: "Meet me at Tom's. Now."

CHAPTER 31

At Tom's the plywood still covered the broken window. Three men sat at a booth waiting for me. My brother had joined the party. I slid in next to him and shook everyone's hand.

Ed lifted his coffee mug in a toast. "Partner, I apologize. Your gut had it right; I was going for the easy conviction. Forgive me?"

I paused and nodded.

"I didn't get called to this meeting so we could get all warm and fuzzy, did I?" Hesidence said. "My office has picked up a lot of chatter across the Middle East. We think something big is going down, but we don't know where. I need your help in shaking all the trees to see what fruit falls out."

"What do you have so far?" asked Ed.

"Like I said, not much. Like Jude, I have a gut feeling this is where it's going to happen. My best summation is that the terrorist networks have too much at stake here. They're getting rid of people who know too much. That includes the three of you."

"I guess I have some information I need to share." For the second time that morning, I retold my visit to Reverend Lamb. "After a bullet narrowly missed his head, he walked the sawdust trail and suddenly believed my warning that his life was in danger. I imagine by now he's at the airport, trying to get out of town."

"He won't go far," Hesidence said. "I put him on the no-fly

list. He'll be arrested and brought to my temporary command center. Did he say anything we need to know?"

"Nothing to go on except that the killers didn't consult Lamb and Amin before Miller's death. The order came from a higher source." I pulled the digital recorder from my pocket. "I have it all here, but there still isn't enough to set Charlie free."

Zach looked at me and asked, "How did you get him to talk?"

"It was one of those 'come to Jesus' sort of discussions." I smiled as I handed the recorder to Hesidence.

Hesidence pocketed it and stood. "Let me get Charlie out of jail. I still have a few friends in this town. Then I'll go have my own talk with the reverend. We need to come up with a lead that tells us what is going to happen next." Hesidence dropped a twenty on the table. A bloody smear streaked across Jackson's face on the bill. I had a momentary flashback to the fire in Cleveland and the blood I left behind on the money I gave to the homeless friend who saved me.

Grinning and shaking my head, I picked up the bill, then looked up at Hesidence. "Where are the other five twenties?"

"You're a good detective, Cameron. Anytime you get tired of that old dog across from you, give me a call." He laughed and walked out of the restaurant.

The three of us stayed for an early lunch. I filled Zach in on Mom's dinner date. Tension from the current situation was showing on my brother's face. He needed the laugh it gave him.

Ed chuckled at the story, but quickly became serious as he caught me up on the police station. "It seems that Captain Seeger left the office early this morning and hasn't been back. And he isn't responding to phone calls. Do you think he could have been involved in this mess?" Ed asked.

"That worries me. He's a good cop. Has anyone gone over to his house to check on him?"

"I thought you might want to join me when I make that house

call."

I smiled and nodded. It felt good to have my partner back.

After we finished lunch, I climbed into Ed's favorite off-duty vehicle, his ancient red pickup truck, and we rattled over the potholes as we drove to the captain's house.

Relief washed over me when I saw the captain's cruiser in the driveway.

We hustled to the door, and Ed knocked. No answer.

He called out, "Captain Seeger!" but still no answer.

At a nod from Ed, we drew our guns. Ed kicked in the door, and we entered cautiously. In the silence, I heard my own breathing and my rapid heartbeat.

Two gun blasts came from the kitchen at the back of the house. The bullets snapped the plaster loose above my head.

Ed and I dove for cover. I went to the floor, and Ed leaped through the doorway to the living room, behind the sofa, just before we heard the back door slam shut. Ed scrambled to his feet, looked around the corner quickly, and then looked at me. He shot me a quick half smile. I knew what that meant.

CHAPTER 32

"Check for the Captain," Ed said as he raced into the hallway toward the kitchen straight ahead. "I'm after this one."

Instead of checking, I followed him as he crashed through the partly open back door at full speed. He got two steps onto the porch before another shot rang out. The shooter leaped over the backyard fence. He was getting away. Such an inept shot—he wasn't the Nightstalker. I shrugged him off.

Ed had fallen backwards in the doorway, sprawled face-up on the floor. He looked up at me and grimaced. "Did you ever wonder if these vests really worked? I know they do—but, man, it hurts. I feel like George Foreman punched me in the chest." He waved a hand toward the house. "Now, go find the Captain."

"Not until you're safe." I pulled him into the kitchen before clearing the first floor of the house room by room.

Quietly climbing the stairs to the second floor, I swung into each room with my gun in the lead. My guess was that the captain was locked in his bathroom. When I called his name, he pulled the door open. In spite of his bloody and swollen face, he could still smile. "I never thought I'd be glad to see you, Cameron."

After calling 911 and telling the operator we had an officer down and needed an ambulance and a squad car, I asked, "What happened? Who's after you? Was it about the Deets case?"

"Partially, yes. What makes you think it's that?"

I shook my head.

He dabbed a washcloth against his split lip and winced. "The mayor's been pushing hard on me to put this case to rest and to make sure you eased off of it. That little weasel threatened my job. Now this. I was glad to help when it looked like we had an open-and-shut case, but everything that's been going on lately got me thinking, so I asked for the folder on the case."

I nodded. "That must have set off an alarm with somebody."

Seeger shook his head. "How anyone knew I was reviewing the case is beyond me."

"There has to be a mole inside the precinct," I offered as I helped him out of the bathroom and down the hall.

Seeger grimaced with pain as I helped him down the stairs. Ed had already gotten to his feet and struggled to the front door. He leaned against the porch's wooden pillars as a black and white and an ambulance rolled up.

I gripped Seeger's shoulder. "You should be fine, Captain." Although he was going to be hurting from the looks of his swollen eyes and blood-splattered clothes.

As the paramedics pulled their stretcher from the vehicle, Seeger looked over at me and said, "I'd like to put you back on the case, Jude, but it has to be unofficial. We don't need anyone asking additional questions. But you could, as a rogue cop gone bad. Right, Dirty Harry?" He tried to smile again, but pain turned it into a scowl.

"There's something to be said for going rogue." I meant it as a joke, but I knew he was talking about the crack house raid. I guess I'd been more obvious than I thought. I shrugged. Probably I was a lousy rogue cop.

CHAPTER 33

Lamb knew Jude Cameron was right. His involvement would either lead him to prison or to death. He was in way over his head. If the forces behind Amin killed Miller because he knew too much, then what would stop them from killing him too?

This wasn't what he'd signed up for. He opened his locked file cabinet, grabbed papers he knew would incriminate him, and forced them into his briefcase. Then he bolted toward the Lexus.

Lamb left dust flying as he raced from the parking lot. He blew through a stop sign and nearly hit a mini-van, but he barely noticed the narrow miss. His mind was on his impending peril.

He'd wanted the money. It was a simple as that. Just the money. He had spent every penny he had to keep his string of small, poor churches floating. His sacrifices were never enough for congregants in those churches. There was always some holier-than-thou, meddlesome group of old ladies that pushed to have him discharged. He was tired of the struggles. He was tired of the church politics that kept him poor and struggling.

When he'd accepted the offer to pastor in Pittsburgh from Amin, his old associate in Cleveland, he saw it as a new start. He'd had to let Amin funnel some money through the church, but it wasn't much money. The fact that the pastorship Amin had offered was one of the shining lights in the denomination had been something he couldn't refuse — his chance to be the big-name pastor he'd always dreamed of.

It was supposed to be the place where he could earn the money he needed to care for his wife, buy the big, new car, and build a savings account for the future. The ministry owed him that much.

Murder had never been a part of the equation.

The Lexus screeched to a stop in the driveway of his home. He leaped from the car, nearly running to the house. Rev. Lamb pushed hard through the front door of his large, brick home. The sound of the door slamming against the wall reverberated through the three-story foyer as he huffed up the stairs with gasping breaths.

His wife rushed from the kitchen. "Honey, why are you home?" She called up the stairs. "What's going on? Is something wrong?" But he never answered.

In the bedroom, he grabbed his passport and the steel strong box filled with hundred-dollar bills from the back corner of the top closet shelf. He needed enough so he could lie low in some other city for a few weeks.

His wife walked in as he turned to go.

"I can't talk now. I'll call when I get where I'm going and let you know I'm safe." His words came out in quick half-breaths.

"Bertrand, you're scaring me. What's going on?" She crossed her arms over her chest. "I'm your wife, and I deserve to know."

"Amin has gotten me into a lot of trouble. I think someone has been hired to kill me."

Her arms dropped to her sides and her mouth dropped open, but he cut off her questions before she could ask any.

"I don't have time to tell you more." He popped open the strong box, pulled several hundred thousand dollars out, and stuck the cash in his coat pocket. The rest of the box he threw at his wife. "Take this and go to see somebody. Not one of the kids. Get out of town. I'll contact you as soon as I can. Don't ask any questions. Right now, knowledge is getting people killed."

He stormed past her and scurried down the stairs. He didn't bother to shut the front door before running to the car. He took one last look at her staring after him from the door, bewildered.

As he threw the luggage into the trunk, she crumpled, tears streaming down her face.

Lamb raced to the airport, still unsure where to go, but whatever plane was leaving soonest would be good enough. He could make another move later on, but right now, he just needed distance between himself, the hired killer, and the police.

As he pulled into the airport's long-term parking lot, red and blue lights flashed behind him. The blue vehicle didn't look like a cop car, but the flashing lights and his excessive speed could only mean one thing: he was going to get a ticket. At least no one would try to kill him with a cop right next to him.

As Lamb searched the glove compartment for his registration and insurance card, he heard a tap on the window. He turned to see the smiling face of a man with a long beard and toothy grin. He shouted, "Allahu akbar!" then pulled the trigger on his pistol.

CHAPTER 34

"The search for Lamb is over." Ed's voice on my phone stopped me in my tracks. "They found him at the airport with his head blown off. Whoever these people are, they don't waste any time whacking witnesses. I've been assigned to interview Lamb's wife. Do you want to come along?"

Sure I did. "I'll meet you at his house, but you'd better let me do the talking. This is going to take a little finesse, and that's something God didn't give you when you were born."

"You know what I got to say to you, Preacher's Kid, and it ain't something you learned in Sunday school."

I chuckled at Ed's old joke as I pulled out my keys, jumped in the car and drove to the address he gave me. When I arrived, the front door stood wide open. The empty house looked suspicious, and my better judgment told me to wait for back-up. But my better judgment didn't always win out. My Dirty Harry persona kicked in, and I drew my weapon.

I pressed my back against the wall by the side of the door and called out, "Is anyone home? This is the police."

No one answered, but footsteps echoed from the upstairs hallway. "Mrs. Lamb? Are you in there?"

No answer.

I saw an office door standing open about four feet down the hall on the left. I'd dive down the hallway, roll into the room, then take cover inside the office somewhere. If the footsteps I heard were the Nightstalker's, the sounds I just made would draw his fire, but my position wouldn't leave me exposed.

I dove for the open door, but the hardwood floors must have just been waxed, and I slid past. A bullet crashed into the frame of the front door. A second one kicked up splinters in the hardwood just behind me. But I couldn't tell my enemy's location because I myself was moving.

Once I stopped sliding, I spun my body into the office and then wiped a bead of sweat from my eye. The narrow escape left my heart beating hard.

I needed to draw his fire again in order to locate him for a kill shot. From the sounds of creaking floor above me I knew he had moved.

"For some kind of hotshot assassin, you are one lousy aim. Where did you learn to shoot, some Al Qaida Boy Scout camp?" Two more splintering bullet holes cracked the floor. The guy was getting closer, and that told me he was on the upstairs' landing. But I didn't want to stand in the hall where he could see me.

"Standard operating procedure, you cowboy!" Ed yelled from outside the front door. "You were supposed to wait for back-up."

"Call it in, old man. I think we have Lamb's killer cornered upstairs," I yelled back.

Two more shots hit the wall near the front door, but the bricks kept Ed safe. The next two shots splintered more floorboards by me.

"You missed again." I taunted the assassin. "Why don't you step out where I can see you, so I can escort you to paradise and you can meet your twelve virgins?"

"Allah promises seventy-two virgins, infidel." The voice came from directly above.

"That's for real men, not little pretend soldiers like you. Sure, you're great at killing old men and women. I bet you even enjoy whacking a kid or baby. But I have bad news for you. This God-fearing, Christian-reared, Pittsburgh redneck knows what you are, and I'm going to settle the score for all the innocent people you murdered. Now you are the hunted and I am the hunter. You're not going to pull your Jihadi bull in my town. Do you hear me? Not. In. My. Town!" I yelled as I dove from the doorway onto my back, sliding along the floor with both guns aimed upward at the spot his voice had come from.

My bullets ripped through the ceiling above me, seeking their target.

No shots returned my fire. Instead, irregular footsteps headed toward the back of the house. Glass broke. Then silence.

I scrambled to my feet only to see a dark car rev up and speed down the alley. The Nightstalker had dropped into the yard from the second floor and escaped.

Ed entered, and we climbed the stairs cautiously. Mrs. Lamb lay crumpled at the top of the stairs, but she would not be getting up. The assassin had placed two bullets in her head. Blood soaked the carpet around her.

I looked for the bullet holes from my shots where they had punched through the splintered floor and torn the carpet. I saw what I had hoped for: droplets of blood around one of the holes. A bullet had gone through the assassin's shoe. Maybe that would slow him down.

I needed an edge for what I planned, and that might just be the one I needed.

CHAPTER 35

"The love of money is the root of all evil, Jude," my mother said as I sank into the chair next to her bed.

"I totally agree, Mom," I replied softly, and I fingered the Powerball tickets in my pocket—my retirement plan if I lived long enough to ever hit the numbers.

"I was sad to hear about Reverend Lamb's wife. I liked her. She was a sweet, godly woman, and she didn't deserve what happened to her. I'm sure she's in Jesus' arms in heaven right now. I'll ask your dad the next time I see him."

"Mom, how did you know about Lamb and his wife? It just happened a few hours ago. The newspapers and TV stations haven't even reported it yet." I pressed her like a prosecuting attorney.

She covered her mouth with both hands and giggled.

"King Solomon again?"

She bobbed her head up and down. "He is such a wise man, Jude. You really need to meet him one day." This time I just nodded. Whoever King Solomon was, he seemed to know more and sooner than anyone else. He had a pipeline. No, several pipelines. Mom was right. I really did need to meet him.

"Did he have another verse for me?"

"Yes," Mom answered me. "'Rejoice not when thine enemy falleth, and let not thine heart be glad when he stumbleth.' That's Proverbs 24:17. He said you'll face your enemy, and he will fall.

When he stumbles, he is more dangerous than when he runs. But when he finally falls, that's not the end. There is a bigger enemy that is greater who you cannot see." Mom repeated Solomon's words with a lucidity that shocked me.

"Wow, that's all pretty deep. I guess I'm being schooled in the wisdom of Solomon. Tell him I appreciate his efforts and I'm listening."

"Good, now be a good boy and go down to the restaurant and get me an Ensure. Just knock on the door and say—"

"Yoo-hoo," I finished. We both laughed. I got her Ensure, kissed her goodbye, and headed back to my apartment to get some sleep. Getting shot at was wearing me out.

Sleep came in fits. New alarms secured my apartment, but I still didn't rest well. After hours of tossing and turning, I finally relaxed and dropped into a deep sleep.

I felt a hand firmly grip my shoulder and shake me.

"Get up, boy. This is the day the Lord has made!"

I knew the voice, and I knew the phrase. That was how Dad woke me up every day of my life.

But Dad was dead. How could he be here shaking me awake?

Whoever it was could be looking down the barrel of pistol. I whipped my gun from under the covers and pointed it at the soft light glowing in my bedroom. The image sharpened, and it was unmistakably my father.

"All this shooting has you a little on edge," Dad said with one of his deep, baritone laughs. "I just thought I would check on you. You need to be more careful. You've got that jihadi guy from Detroit so mad at you that he's willing to put some lead in you for free. What did you say to him to make him so angry?"

"Are you for real?" I rubbed my eyes. I felt awake. My eyes tried to focus, but like in a dream, I couldn't capture the whole image. Yet I was aware of his presence.

"That's for you to figure out, little man. I suppose it could be just memories that pop out, like buds on trees in the springtime. It could be a lot of things, but you can make up your own mind. In the meantime, I came to check on you." He smiled as he stood. "That's what dads do."

"Uh, yeah, Dad." Further words deserted me.

"Many reasons led to the choice to involve you. One is your faith. That has been a little sketchy lately, but you did tell that assassin guy you were a God-fearing, Christian-reared man." He barrel-laughed at his own joke, standard as his humor.

Abruptly, the laughter stopped. Dad leaned closer. His image sharpened. Dad stared down at me with a look that made me squirm now as much as it had when I was growing up. "Maybe you're starting to see the big picture. Do you know what Proverbs 22:6 says?"

My overwhelmed brain couldn't process the request. "Sword drills in the middle of the night by a deceased relative aren't a strong point for me."

Dad barrel-laughed again.

I was starting to like this dream. Maybe I could catch up on my sleep after this was all over, and Dad and I could go fishing in a future dream. His larger than life persona had invaded my dreams ever since childhood. I wished deeply that I had him back.

"You got your sense of humor from me. The verse says, 'Train up a child in the way he should go, and when he is old he will not depart from it.' I always knew that whatever you went through, you would return to the Lord. That's why He chose you," Dad said. He started to fade.

"Who chose me, and for what?" I tried to throw off the blankets as I reached out to grab my father's fading form. His face dimmed into the darkness, followed by one last word: "This."

The next thing I knew, light cut through the blinds, and my phone was ringing. I fumbled for it on the bedside table.

"Cameron here."

"You don't know me, but we need to talk," said a voice I didn't recognize.

CHAPTER 36

Captain Seeger had returned to work after a day off following his near-death experience at the hands of the Nightstalker. Palms sweaty, he opened his door and spoke to his assistant.

"Did you set my press conference for tomorrow?"

"Done, Captain."

"You didn't tell anyone else, did you? I want to make sure that what I say is heard from me first." The words came out in a stutter. His eyes darted from face to face in the squad room.

After the attempt on his life, Seeger planned to make things right by telling what he knew. His only protection would be if the press knew his part of the story — his part in the distasteful political mess.

"No, sir."

Seeger stepped closer to her desk and lowered his voice. "Call Rivers and Cameron. Tell them to meet me tonight in the Strip District across from Wholey's at midnight." Seeger looked from side to side to make sure no one else could have overheard him, then he moved back into his office and shut the door.

* * *

His assistant waited a few minutes until Seeger was on the phone. She dialed a private line at the mayor's office.

"This is Cal."

"Seeger's press conference is set for nine a.m. tomorrow. He also wanted me to contact Rivers and Cameron to meet him at midnight tonight." She reported what her boss had told her in a whisper.

"Thank you. I'll pass this on to the mayor. He'll take care of the details. Don't call Rivers. I have reason not to trust him, but leave a message on Cameron's office extension.

"By the way, your promotion to the City Hall position was just approved, as I promised it would be. In fact, the mayor would like you to be a part of the welcoming ceremony for the first lady. I'll email the details to you."

The news made her want to shout, but she allowed herself only a mental pat on the back. She'd made the right choice, accepting the proposal the mayor's Chief of Staff offered.

* * *

Newspaper folded neatly under his arm, Cal sauntered through the park to a bench overlooking one of the three rivers that joined together in Pittsburgh, where Rafi waited for him. He imitated his fellow jihadist by opening the paper and using it to hide his moving lips so no surveillance cameras could see what they were saying. The two appeared to be businessmen escaping the doldrums of daily office life by slipping out to the park for a private moment. "Captain Seeger is going to blow the top off the mayor's involvement tomorrow at a press conference. We need to eliminate him," Cal said.

"Agreed. We're so close to the Day of Reckoning," Rafi said. "We can't let him compromise the plan. But we can't make it obvious."

"Will the Nightstalker take care of this?"

"No, he's assigned to eliminate Cameron, then leave town. This is a top priority, but Cameron is much more prepared than I expected. He is also getting help from someone, but I don't know who. He knows far too much. I want him eliminated quickly, before he ties this all together. You'll have to take care of Seeger yourself."

Cal swore under his breath, but a plan began to form. "Seeger's assistant was to tell Detective Cameron to meet the captain at midnight tonight. I told her to put it on his office extension. Since he's suspended, he'll never hear it. That is, until the District Attorney plays the message for a Grand Jury. With a few more well-planted clues I believe Cameron will be facing a long sentence for killing the captain."

Rafi was quiet for a moment. "Take the mayor along to make sure we have plenty on him, in case we need to force his cooperation on the Day of Reckoning. Make Seeger's killing look scandalous. The press will do what they always do: focus on the scandal and ignore everything else. We should have delivered our greatest blow against the Great Satan by the time anyone digs deeper or discovers otherwise."

Cal rustled his newspaper. "Since Detective Cameron would be tied to the killing, that will add one more thing to his growing list of problems. Habibi will make sure everyone who knows our plans or can connect us together is eliminated on the Day of Reckoning. In the meantime, we must misdirect."

CHAPTER 37

The usual sounds filled the Baptist Senior Home that morning. The screamer stood in the hallway, shouting unintelligible, guttural sounds. Bird Lady talked to the parakeets, and the home's phones rang nonstop. A normal day, but I hoped my visit with Mom would be abnormal.

I wasn't sure when King Solomon communicated to her as the days went by, but his guiding verse had been right on the money each time. I hoped for something else that would give me a break in this confusing mess.

"Good morning, Mom," I said as I strolled through the door.

She looked up over her smudged glasses with a smile. "He's not the author of confusion."

I bit. "Who isn't the author of confusion?"

"God. Oh, Jude, you know that, but King Solomon thought I should remind you of that fact. He's worried about your crisis of faith." Mom plopped her slight body onto her bed.

"What makes him think I'm having a crisis of faith?" I should have known better, but I asked anyway.

"Your dad's illness and death and my illness rocked your world. I know that. Your dad knows it. So does King Solomon. Now, this new puzzle is confusing you. I think it's time for you to rely on God. You need to trust Him again. Would you pray with me?" Her eyes pleaded with me as she held out her hands.

These lucid moments from my mother confused me more

than anything else. How she bounced in and out of dementia, I had no idea. Prayer was the last thing I wanted, but her words rang true.

"Sure, Mom. I'd like that." I said the words half to prevent an argument and half because she was right.

"Like what, Jude?" The dementia plunged in behind her eyes.

The light that had shimmered in her gaze since I was a child only occasionally shone in the present. My dear, sweet mother was escaping, and there was nothing I could do about it.

"Nothing, Mom. Did you talk to King Solomon lately?"

"My, my, my, I have had such a busy morning with guests. It's been one after another. Your dad and Deacon Miller came in at sunrise, but they didn't stay long. Your dad had a message for you, and I promised him I would pass it on."

Mom reached for her Ensure. After her story about the restaurant and shouting yoo-hoo, she continued. "I don't understand the meaning of what your dad said, so don't ask me. I just don't know." She stopped again and took another sip before finishing. "Your father said to tell you, 'There are three.'" She shrugged. "Like I told you, I don't know what it means, so don't shoot the piano player."

"The phrase is 'Don't shoot the messenger.' You mean 'messenger,' don't you, Mom?"

"Don't correct your mother, young man," she said lightly. "It's my story, and I'll tell it the way I want. After your dad and Deacon Miller left, King Solomon and I had breakfast together."

"Were his wives there?"

"He had them all over the place. Look, there goes one now." She pointed into the hallway.

One of the nurse's aides walked by and winked at my mother.

"Did you see that? She's jealous. Why would she be jealous of an old broad like me?" Mom smiled at her joke and added, "Then again, I am quite a hottie." She started laughing one of

148

her hearty laughs that always rolled through each room of our house as we were growing up. Even if Dad told her an old joke, she would laugh.

"What did King Solomon tell you?" There was no time for much prodding, and I was starting to lose her.

"Chapter one, verse eight. It was one of my favorites. It says, 'My son, hear the instruction of thy father, and forsake not the law of thy mother.' Listen to what your father tells you." She scooted off the bed. "I have to run down to the gym for my yoga class. I have to keep my trim, girlish figure. I have a lot of wives to compete with." Mom giggled and put on her slippers.

"I need to get going anyway." True, but I also wanted to avoid the story of George, the guy from Germany who sent her gifts.

As I stood up, Mom looked at me and said, "The expression is, 'Don't shoot the piano player.' You, Jude, are the messenger. King Solomon said so."

CHAPTER 38

I had to meet Hesidence at Tom's Diner before my secretive meeting with my mysterious caller, who told me nothing more than where to meet and when. It was the first piece of business I told Hesidence about, the only sane piece of information I could give him. I was reluctant to talk about my dream—or whatever it was—when I spoke to my dad, and my mother's dream about my dad, but I did anyway.

"You sure do live an exciting life after bedtime, Jude. I don't know how to read all of that. Let's try to break it into pieces. Your enemy is this Nightstalker guy, and according to Rivers, you really got under his skin."

He leaned back and shook his head. "As weird as it is, I think your dad is right. You've been chosen for this. I don't know why, but everything seems to circle back around to you. Think back. Who have you really, really ticked off?"

"No one's threatened my life since Afghanistan."

"What happened there?"

"I had to take out some kid who thought he was invincible. It turned out his brother was some tribal chieftain or something like that. He sent an entire Taliban group out after me." I stirred my coffee.

"I take it from the fact that you're here, it didn't work. Well, I doubt if that's what's behind all this. Remember, Al Qaida has been decimated and the Taliban is on the run." He snickered. No one in the intelligence divisions or the military believed it, but it was what was told to the citizens of the United States.

He looked out the broken window, now fixed. "Seriously, I don't think some Taliban chieftain has the reach, even if he has the desire, to pay back old debts so far away."

I shook my head and shrugged. "I can't think of who or what right now." I lifted my cup of coffee for a sip. "Back to the visit my mother had from my dad. What do you think the word three means?"

"Don't know, but keep that number in your head. So far, everything King Solomon's told you has been on the nose. I'm sure it will come in handy at the right moment. I've gotta go. I have to oversee the first lady's visit to Pittsburgh in two days. I may be hard to reach until this babysitting duty is done. Be careful, and watch your step." Hesidence laid another blood-smeared twenty on the table.

It made me think. The first lady was coming. Is that why he was here? Why had he been watching me? More importantly, what did he know that he wasn't telling me?

I decided to stay and have a late lunch at Tom's and try to figure it out before meeting with my mystery phone caller from the morning. I should be concerned about walking into a trap. Nightstalker had been unable to finish his job, and this could be a way to catch me unaware, yet something in her grave voice exuded a true need for my help. Maybe I was a fool though.

I wanted back-up, but Ed or Hesidence would only scare the caller away. Maybe Zach, but he...well, he was an accountant. Zach was no killer, assassin, or even a street brawler. I decided to forgo the back-up. Instead, I pulled out my phone and typed out a text to Zach.

Meeting someone with info I need. 10:00 @ the N Park Lodge.

The lodge was both quiet and out of the way. That would worry Zach, but I knew it well enough to strategically place myself for safety.

I reached in my pocket, pulled out the paperback Bible, and started to read from the Book of Proverbs. Maybe it was time to look for some insight or knowledge inside the words that had been spoon-fed to me by my mother's very secretive beau, King Solomon.

I skipped through the verses in the Wisdom of Solomon. In the back of my mind I saw the lifeless bodies of Rev. Lamb and his wife. They most likely knew or had read the verses I skimmed, but allowed their truths to be dislodged from their moral compass.

As the waitress topped off my cooling coffee, I found myself reading Chapter Sixteen. I ran a finger down through the verses until I got to verse thirty. The words spoke to me like they used to speak to my father when I was a kid. He would slam his hand down on his massive, leather Bible and then jump up, dance around, and shout, "Praise the Lord! There's the answer, my little Jude. God has given me the answer. It is as plain as day." Then he would dance around some more.

I read the passage softly aloud, "There is a way that seemeth right unto a man, but the ends thereof are the ways of death." That was my answer. When Lamb chose to do what seemed right to him, he set himself on the path that led to his own death. This hadn't been the judgment of a wicked and angry God, simply the outcome of a bad choice.

I got up from the table at Tom's and closed the worn cover of the Bible. I could still remember my father presenting it to me during a warm, summer Sunday morning service. I was graduating to the Middle School age group in our Sunday school with a perfect attendance record.

"Let it be your guide, Jude," he'd said in both a proud and wise tone.

A voice spoke from behind me in the diner. "You just had a

praise-the-Lord moment, didn't you, son?"

I smiled to myself and turned to face an old man. He smiled at me with a near-toothless grin. Lines etched his face, but not one of them seemed to be from worry. These were all marks of joy, sergeant stripes of jubilation.

Before I said a word, he said, "I knew it." A radiance seemed to expand beyond his face. "Last time I saw and felt that comin' from someone was the last time I talked to my preacher. Course that man of God has gone on to his reward, but he taught me to watch for it. Are you a preacher, son?"

I laughed. "Far from it. I'm just a cop."

"Too bad, 'cause the Lord has anointed you. Your mamma must be praying for you. I will, too." The old man put a hand on either side of my face. "God's got some work for you to do, and He's laboring hard over your life. You better listen." Some type of electricity moved from him to me.

"God is calling you back to Him, son. He wants you to be His messenger. Are you ready to surrender?"

"I still have some baggage to unpack before I settle back into church, but do keep praying for me. I can use it right now." I patted his shoulder and moved past him to the door.

"Wait a second, son. God doesn't talk to me like this very often, but when He does, I need to say everything He tells me to say. And He wants me to tell you that there are three. That's all He said. I guess you know what He's talking about."

"Not yet, but I have a feeling I will when the time is right. Thanks again for your prayers." I smiled my own version of a wide, toothy grin and left.

I felt like I was living in Mom's world. Everything coincided, but nothing made sense. I looked back at the old man, but he was gone. Probably went to the restroom, that's all. Nothing more than that.

CHAPTER 39

I arrived at North Park Lodge early to walk the perimeter of the old building, which was set on a hill at the end of a long, winding road with several hundred feet of open fields on three sides. Anyone arriving could be heard driving up the steep slope.

I walked down the line of trees along the fourth side of the Lodge, searching for any sign of someone making plans to eliminate me. Even the pathways looked untouched. I worked my way around to the lower back patio, where I had asked my caller to meet me, and which gave me even more protection.

I was standing in the dark shadows with my back to the stone wall when the chugging of an engine climbed the hill as an unseen car drove toward the lodge. In a few moments, a slim, female figure rounded the corner of the building. I recognized her right away, even though it was dark and she was dressed in black leather: Lamb's former secretary.

I pulled my gun and steadied it before speaking. "I thought you were dead."

She turned toward my voice. "You can put that down. I came to ask for your help before I fulfill your prophecy of my death." She slowly reached into a holster strapped under her coat and slid out a pistol. With two fingers, she held it up for a moment so I could see it in the moonlight. "I am placing my gun down on the table."

"Why should I believe you, and why shouldn't I just put a

bullet in you right now?" My tension and anger seeped into my voice.

She didn't respond. Instead, she backed several steps away from the table.

I rushed forward and placed the barrel of my gun to her temple. With my free hand, I carefully frisked her for other weapons. She was dangerous at any distance, even more so when I was this close. My pat-down was quick but thorough, and my gun never left her head.

When I found no weapons, I removed my gun from her head but didn't put it away. It was time to talk, but there was no need to be foolish.

"I know they got Lamb and his wife," she said. "I know there are two more targets, and both are standing right here. That is why I called you. I want to surrender, but you can't take me to jail. The people who brought me here have associates inside your police force. In fact, they have associates a lot further up the chain than you can imagine." She took a seat at the picnic table and gazed sadly out at the playground with legs swinging as if she was lost in a memory of her childhood.

I towered over her. "They won't offer you immunity. You'll end up doing hard time for all that you've done, and I have feeling I don't know even a portion of it. Surely you knew that already, so why would you trust me?"

"If there is anything I learned in the last few days, it is that you are a good man...and very smart. You can make this all work, and I know you'll keep your word. Once I'm in custody, the information I have will be worth quite a bit to some parts of your government, and bring down other parts. Those parts will, and do, want me silenced. Right now, you are the only one I trust."

I scratched my head, but couldn't help myself. What a turnabout. "How do I know your information is good? Give me some proof." I positioned myself between her and her pistol.

"No can do. Take me to someone who can make a deal. I have one thing to take care of tonight, and then I will meet you first thing in the morning."

My gut told me that she had info that might bring this jigsaw puzzle of a mystery together. Why not surrender now? I mused. She might be testing the waters.

"Give me something that will get the feds interested. I need a little if I'm going to be the go-between," I told her.

The Black Rose stood and looked out over the swing sets below us. She sighed, and when she turned back unshed tears glistened in the moonlight. "When I was a Sunni child in the Middle East, Shi'a rebels came through our town and took all our parents to the local playground. There they lined them up in front of us children and executed them. I vowed then to fight back. I have fought back, and I am good at it. Children should not have to watch their parents die." She paused and drew a long breath. "And parents should never have to watch their children die."

She turned away again and started to walk around the building to her car. "I will call you in the morning and give you the location of where I am hiding." She disappeared around the corner, without even trying to retrieve her pistol.

The engine revved to life, then rumbled away from the lodge into the cool, wintry evening.

I cautiously made my way along the tree line to my car, confident that no one saw us or heard our conversation.

On the way home, I dialed Hesidence's number. "Jack, the Black Rose is still alive. She wants me to bring her in, and has information that will probably blow the lid off this case. Call me back when you get this."

CHAPTER 40

Cal glanced at the under-aged hooker in the back of his car. Under the influence of the barbiturates he had provided her as payment for her services, she sat quietly and asked no questions.

He pulled the car over to the side of the road a couple of blocks away from the spot where Captain Seeger would be waiting for Jude to appear at midnight. But it wouldn't be Jude who would show up. He drove to an alley where he could see Seeger waiting in the shadows. He chuckled at the thought of the scandal that his arrangements would bring about.

Cal looked over at the mayor in the seat beside him and spoke calmly, "Did you bring your weapon like I asked?"

The mayor nodded and pulled the gun from his pocket with a slight protest. "I don't know why you wanted me to bring it. We're just setting him up for a scandal that will ruin him, right?"

Cal scooped it off the console between them and twisted a silencer on the end. The mayor's eyes were opening to the real plan but, as with many things Cal did, the mayor was a few steps behind.

The Strip District hopped during the day with workers and shoppers but echoed with emptiness in this remote section at night. Cal rolled the car up to Seeger and pushed the button to lower the tinted window.

The captain read the tea leaves quickly. He reached into his coat, probably for his service revolver, but Cal didn't wait to find out.

Seeger's eyes widened as the mayor's chief of staff pulled the trigger, but only for a split second. The captain's body pulsed backwards before falling to the alley cement.

Surprise and shock ran across the mayor's face.

Cal stepped out of the car and checked the captain's vitals. He nodded congratulations to himself. He still had it, Cal thought. He could still kill with the best of them. Seeger was shot right between the eyes. Cal strolled back to the car and peered in at the Mayor, showing him the pistol in his hand.

The mayor's brow furrowed and then he blinked.

Cal let a smile cross his face. It was the mayor's gun. The man had just realized he'd been framed for the murder of a Pittsburgh police captain. The mayor and Officer Cameron, in cahoots. It was delicious. That would be the story if Mayor Budding didn't follow along as instructed.

Cal moved to the back door of the black sedan, opened it, and grabbed the young prostitute by the hair, pulling her across the smooth, soft leather seat. He roughly stood her up about four feet from the captain's dead body. He ripped open her blouse and steadied her.

"Stand still. Do not move or things will get bad for you," Cal said near her ear.

The mayor closed his eyes and turned away, tears running down his cheeks.

Cal reached a gloved hand under Seeger's coat. The top cop hadn't even cleared leather before the bullet went through his brain. Cal removed the revolver, turned toward the girl, and fired one shot to her heart. She collapsed in a lump. He placed the gun in Seeger's hand, stepped over the girl, got back in the car and calmly drove away.

After a moment the mayor spoke. "Cal, you just murdered two people. What's going on?"

158

"Seeger spilled the beans on you, as they say. I had to protect you, but to protect me, I used your gun. Now you won't talk about this, and neither will I." Cal held the mayor's gaze.

The mayor brushed away a tear, gave a nod, and then paused. "He's a top cop. They'll do a hard investigation and figure this one out. We'll ride the needle for this."

Cal just smiled, knowing it would rattle the mayor even more. "The investigation will find Captain Seeger next to a minor, and on closer inspection, they will find child porn on his home computer. The department will cover it up rather than look any further into it." He patted his jacket pocket. "In a few weeks, I'll dispose of the gun."

The mayor smiled and relaxed.

Cal, feeling the adrenaline in his bloodstream, punched the accelerator and congratulated himself. Operation Misdirect would occupy the police force until the Day of Reckoning.

CHAPTER 41

No more words passed between the men as the two traveled back to the City Hall offices. As Cal wheeled the car around the corner of the building, he noticed a ray of light glancing a reflective beam off of his office window. He stopped a half block away and turned slowly to Budding. "Someone is snooping around in my office. I want you to wait here while I see who it is."

Budding didn't argue but simply slouched in his seat until he had a good view of the window and its mysterious light.

His aide slipped out of the car and ran down the sidewalk on the other side of the street. He let himself into the side entrance and climbed the stairs to the fifth floor. Budding's office and his own adjoined each other. He let himself into the mayor's office and crossed quietly to the door to his own office.

Cal raised his gun and reached for the doorknob. He slowly turned it. His eyes ran across the office from corner to corner. No one was there. He slowly stepped into the dim room. He reached for his phone to call the mayor to inform him that it was safe to enter.

That moment of distraction was all the Black Rose needed.

She stepped silently from behind the door, placing her semi-automatic pistol at the nape of his neck. "Drop your gun, Cal," she commanded with an edge of ice cracking around the words.

"What do you want, Rose? I can no longer help you. Our leader has decided that you failed your mission. You need to leave now and run as far as you can. I can give you some money."

She jammed the barrel into his neck. "I want the papers that you've been collecting on your mission and I want the photos that most certainly incriminate me. I want it all." She spat the words at the back of his head.

"I don't keep any of that here. I will take you to them. Just back off with the revolver a little. My car is outside and we can get you everything you need. Would you, please, lower your gun?" he pleaded. The Black Rose was a killer, and blowing his brains out would be easy for her. But surely she would keep him alive to get the documents she wanted.

She took a step away from him but did not lower her gun. Cal turned, sighed with slight relief, and his eyes caught a faint, shadowy form passing into the doorway of his office.

Budding stepped silently into the carpeted room and raised a baseball bat, probably the autographed one he kept on a shelf near the door. Budding struck without warning, hitting the small woman in the back of her head. She dropped to the area carpet that covered the office floor.

Cal's heart missed a beat and started again. He pulled Budding's gun from his jacket pocket and finished her off. He turned to see Mayor Budding still standing with the bat but starting to wobble. Taking a life impacted him hard. Cal raced to his side and pulled the bat from his fingers. He guided his boss to a chair where the mayor collapsed into the soft leather.

Cal poured a shot of bourbon from his bar and handed it to Budding. "Drink this to calm your nerves. You have to go home. I will take care of everything. And by the way, thank you for saving my life."

Budding smiled up at him and downed the bourbon. After a moment he pushed himself out of the chair and attempted to stand. Cal looked down at him and said, "Give it another few minutes. Then we will get you out of here."

"I think I'm okay." The mayor stood, wavered, and walked to the door leading into the hallway. As he pulled the door open he looked back at Cal and asked, "You have this covered, right?"

"Covered, boss. Go home and get some sleep." He watched Budding leave the room.

Cal pulled his phone from his pocket again and pressed a speed dial number. A groggy, half-asleep voice answered. "Yes Khaliq, how can I help you?"

"The Black Rose came to visit me, but she has departed for paradise. Pick up Eb and come to my office with the van. Bring your cleaning supplies. Now!" Cal barked. As an afterthought he added, "When you dump her, cut out her tongue. I want it as a warning to all involved."

CHAPTER 42

Morning didn't happen the way I expected. I sat drinking hot coffee in pajamas at the kitchen island when the phone rang. It was Ed Rivers.

His voice crackled in my ear. "Jude, Seeger was killed last night. Uniforms found him with an underage hooker. Both dead in an alley. The detectives think you did it. There's a voicemail on your precinct extension asking you to meet him last night. I hope you have a good alibi."

"Wait a second. You said Seeger is dead? What happened? And yes, I have a good alibi. I was with the woman in black last night. She wants me to bring her in. I think she has information that will answer all our questions. Didn't you see the message I sent you last night?"

"Then it doesn't look good for you, 'cause that mysterious woman in black was found with her tongue cut out and a bullet to her brain. I'm calling to give you a few steps lead on the uniforms heading to your apartment now. Get out of there! We'll find the real killer, but right now, you're number one on the suspect list, and there isn't any two, three or four unless they're all you."

I darted into the bedroom, grabbed my clothes from the day before, pulled them on, leaped down the steps two at a time, and started my car. I had no idea where to go. Worse, I needed another car to get there. Whose?

I dialed Zach. "Hey, brother, I need a favor."

"How can I help, Jude?"

"I want to switch cars with you for a few days. I've been accused of Captain Seeger's murder and need to travel incognito."

There was a bit of silence as Zach processed this, but he said, "My wife and kids took the car when they went into hiding. All I have is the minivan. That'll cramp your style, but—"

My call waiting beeped, and I checked caller ID. "Hesidence is on the other line," I told Zach. "I'll call you back after I see what he has to say." I pushed the button to take the call. "This is Jude."

"Where are you? We need to meet now."

"Heading toward Zach's to switch cars."

"Forget it. He's under surveillance. Meet me at that basketball court where you nearly got yourself killed. Go there now. Don't stop for anyone."

He went on, talking fast. "I suppose you already heard your friend, Lamb's secretary, codename Black Rose, got whacked last night. I need to have all the information you have from your meeting with her. And I need it quick. Something big is going down, and I don't have time to waste while the Pittsburgh police ties up my one good source of information."

I jammed my foot on the gas. The decaying buildings and back streets echoed with the roar of the engine and whining gears. I expected to pick up a black-and-white as I raced up and down the hills, but none were in sight.

I downshifted then braked to a stop at the basketball court. Hesidence's Suburban waited for me. A tinted window lowered, and he motioned me to get in with him. His eyes darted from a stack of papers to the computer screen next to him. His brow was furrowed with an increasing frown, and his casual stance and relaxed good nature had disappeared.

"I hope you have something good to add to this puzzle. I've been running down what I assumed must be rabbit trails for days now." His words came out sharp and clipped. "I thought they all led to different places. Now I'm almost certain they're linked. I hope you can give me something that ties it all together." He blew out a frustrated breath.

"First of all," I said, "You know someone murdered Seeger last night, and that I am suspect numero uno. The Black Rose was going to give us that common cord that runs through this whole mess. She led me to believe it all linked together from Amin to Lamb to Orval Miller when she hinted that this went far up the law enforcement and political food chains. We're on the right track, but I don't have any answers."

"Tell me exactly what she said."

I reviewed the whole conversation. Once I finished, I told him, "As she was ready to leave, I asked for a little taste, just enough to convince you she had something good to offer. She stared over at the swing-sets, then told a story from her childhood about watching Shi'a rebels kill her parents. She said it was a horrible thing that no child should have to see. Then she added that no parent should have to watch their child be killed either. She walked away after that."

"I don't know what that means. What could her moment of tenderness have to do with this?" Hesidence blew out another very frustrated breath, his words laced with a tint of irony.

"It relates, but I haven't put my finger on it." I shook my head. I felt his frustration and wished I had more to go on. It seemed all I had was a bunch of isolated bits and pieces.

"Something else I keep hearing in the chatter on the Internet is 'The Day of Reckoning.' We don't know where, and we don't know what, but it feels big...." Hesidence stared out the window in silence.

Just when I thought he was done, he turned back to me, leaned forward as though sharing a great secret, and looked into my eyes. "I'm going to need your help, Jude. The first lady is coming to town, and the president wants me on her detail. It's irregular, and I'm sure the Secret Service doesn't want me there and has their panties in a bunch over it. So, for the next twenty-four hours, I have to make that my top priority. I need you to go out and solve all these bits and pieces. Let me get through tomorrow morning, and we'll work on this together. Until then, you'll have to be my lead on this."

"It might be hard with all of Pittsburgh's men in blue searching for me, and a foreign assassin trying to put my head on his trophy wall, but I'll do what I can," I said.

"The Nightstalker is in your court. Take him out, and we can start taking care of the rest. As far as the cops go, I'll call the mayor's office and get him to call off the dogs. He is behind this push to hang everything on you. The guy has a few skeletons in his closet that I will hint about and that should cool his jets for a day or two." Hesidence pushed the door open, my clue to leave and get back to work.

As I exited the Suburban, my phone rang.

"Brother, I thought you were coming here to get the van. I was getting worried."

"I'm sorry, Zach. Hesidence called and we had to meet immediately. He said he'll take care of the police. I won't need your car. Hesidence's got his tentacles into a lot of people. I am praying he can do it quickly. Until then I could use an early lunch. How about pizza?"

"I can meet in an hour. And use the evasive moves I taught you when we were kids just in case Hesidence can't get the boys in blue off our backs. Will that be all right with you?"

"Yeah, I'll stop by and see Mom, then." I knew I had to sneak in from behind the building, but no one knew the area, the alleys, and the bike paths better than I did.

"Tell her that her favorite son says hello, and maybe she'll introduce you to her boyfriend." He chuckled as he hung up.

CHAPTER 43

Mom wasn't in her room. Panic hit me. I had no idea what this Nightstalker was willing to do to get to me. A cold sweat broke on my brow as I hurried out the door and down the hall. I asked at the nurse's station where she was, and they looked at each other with puzzled expressions. The one with spiky blonde hair said, "I was in there less than five minutes ago, and she was in bed. Maybe she slipped into the bathroom. Don't be so paranoid, Jude. Go back and look again."

She was right. I was getting jumpy and paranoid.

When I walked back into the room, Mom exited the bathroom holding a large vase filled with a bouquet of flowers.

"Aren't these lovely?" She held it up so I could get a good view of the beautiful carnations and daisies. "Some people still remember that Edna loves to get flowers," she chided me.

I stood accused and guilty.

"Aren't they beautiful, Jude?" Mom exclaimed. The smile that creased her aging face jotted me a mental note to bring her flowers more often.

"Just like you, Mom. Who gave them to you?" I half expected to hear about her friend George from Germany once again.

"I didn't know him. He was tall, thin, and very dark complected. Middle Eastern-looking is what most people would say."

I clenched my fists, my heart racing, as she settled the flowers

167

on the windowsill. If this was who I suspected then there would double hell to pay.

"He told me he's an old hunting buddy of yours and was hoping I could tell him where you were. I had no idea, so I told him that. I didn't know you took up hunting, Jude." She sat on her bed.

"Just special game. Did he say anything else?"

"Yes, he wants you to meet him at the church around eleven tonight. He says he needs to settle things with you. I have no idea what that means, but I told him I would tell you. I told you, so now I can rest. Tell your brother he needs to visit his mother more often, and that he should bring flowers like your friend." Mom leaned back as her eyes closed. I would get no more from her.

The Nightstalker crossed a line when he visited my mother. Civilians are civilians to a cop, but to a terrorist they're a main target, and the ones easiest to terrorize.

I no more than got to my car when the phone rang. According to my caller ID, it was Izzie. "Hello, is everything all right?" My concern for her filled my voice. Had she received a Middle-Eastern visitor too?

"All is fine with me, but it isn't with my niece. Do you remember that I said Gloria was the only survivor from Amin's last trip to Afghanistan? Well, she was going through her things from the trip and found a chador—a head covering—that the bomber had given her. As she was refolding it she found a note asking for forgiveness. The young man wrote a full page in English, and there might be something in it you'd like to see."

"Absolutely. I'll be outside your building in ten minutes." I quickened my pace to my car.

I dialed Zach to let him know that I would be late but that I still wanted to meet. By the time I finished talking to him I was at Izzie's.

She climbed into the Chevelle and gave me Gloria's house address. We drove there in silence, since my mind was on the Nightstalker and our scheduled rendezvous. I wanted to take him alive, but dead would suit me just fine.

Gloria's mother greeted us and escorted us to the family room off the back. It was quaintly decorated in a country motif with an overabundance of accents. It was too cluttered for me, but I assumed Gloria's mom liked it, no matter what I thought.

A slender, pretty teenager sat with her feet tucked under her on the leather sofa, clutching a black cloth. She stood to greet me.

Izzie handled the introductions. "Gloria, this is Detective Cameron from the Pittsburgh Police Department, here to talk to you about your friend in Afghanistan."

Gloria's face was pensive. "Mahmood was so sweet to all of us, and his last gesture to me was to buy me this chador." She rubbed a hand lightly over the cloth. "He gave me this when he brought me the phone I lost. It was so nice of him to give me a gift when I was so foolish to drop my phone. He told me to watch the video he recorded for me, but it never worked after the explosion."

Izzie nodded. "I felt Detective Cameron needed to read that letter from him. Could he see it for a moment?"

"Here's the letter. You can read it." Gloria placed it in my hand.

Izzie scanned over my shoulder while I read.

Dear Gloria,

Since you are reading this, you know that I have ended the story for your friends and my friends. When the Americans first liberated my country, they brought freedoms and a better life to my family. As they chose to pull out of my country, they left it to be ruled by the Taliban chieftains again, and soon I think it will be overrun by the Islamic State, as in Iraq. In order to feed my family and care for my ill mother, I agreed to work for the Taliban commander, Sabawoon Habibi.

He is producing heroin and will ship it in the caskets of your friends to your hometown to a man I have heard called Amin. Sabawoon is using the money from the heroin to fund a Day of Reckoning jihad against your country. I am not sure of his plans.

I did make a video of their meeting last night on your phone. I did not understand what they were talking about, but someone in your country will understand. Please forgive me and keep the chador to remind you that there is a good man inside me somewhere, and that this good man loved you.

Mahmood

"He sounds like a good man in a very hard situation. Can I take this with me to a friend at the CIA?" I held the letter up. "And if you still have your phone, I think the CIA can get that video off of it. It may have information pertinent to a possible terrorist attack." I intentionally chose vague words. No need to panic anyone.

Her eyes welled with tears. "Yes, if I can help prevent any more deaths, then take them and keep them." She plucked a battered phone from the table and handed it to me.

Izzie and I left quietly as Gloria's tears became sobs and the girl buried her head in her mother's shoulder.

Once back in the car, I called Hesidence to tell him we must meet, and he needed to bring his best video tech.

CHAPTER 44

At the curb in front of Izzie's building, we climbed into Hesidence's Suburban. I glanced around for those who hunted me. No one sat in unmarked cars watching Izzie's door. Hesidence must have used his persuasive skills to call the hounds off my trail, at least for the time being.

He read the letter quickly and passed the phone back to his technician. The young agent started swapping parts and attaching pieces to his laptop as we talked. The vehicle moved slowly around the block.

"I know this Sabawoon guy from Afghanistan," I said. "I mentioned him before. He led a battle against us. In the middle of the battle, his younger brother and I got tied up in a knife fight. The kid was arrogant about his skills, but he obviously didn't know about my neighborhood or my Ranger training. He ended up with his throat cut, and this Habibi guy threatened to kill me if it was the last thing he ever did. Once I got back to the States, I simply dismissed it."

Hesidence sat back and threw his arms behind his head before he spoke. "He's grown much stronger since you left. He's forged relationships with other terrorist groups. He has the power, and obviously, he now has the finances to reach all the way to Pittsburgh. I would have dismissed it if it had been any other tribal leader's brother you killed, but not this guy. Still, I don't think you're his only target. Once we get into the video file,

I hope we'll get an idea of what his plan is, and who's going to pull it off." He sighed. "I feel like I'm standing in the midst of a rushing river but I can't see either shoreline."

"Maybe this is the break we need," I offered.

Hesidence nodded. "Either way, we'll need to keep working, and working harder, to put together all the clues and information we have before something drastic happens."

A serious feeling of foreboding tightened my jaw and soured my mood. We knew who was behind it all. And we knew Amin's fundraising role in the scenario. I tossed out a suggestion to Hesidence. "Should I have Ed Rivers arrest Amin and question him?"

"I thought of that, but if we do then we play our hand before we know enough of the facts." He shook his head. "No, I'm moving an asset to keep a 24/7 vigil on the man. After Lamb's killing, he's most likely frightened to death. If he knew the big picture he would have run to us already, just to save his butt."

I reached for the door handle. "Keep me informed. I have to meet with my brother tonight and then take care of another issue." I decided not to tell Hesidence about my rendezvous with the Nightstalker—he'd try to stop me, and after the assassin's visit with my mother, it had gotten personal, very personal. "I'll be around and can be reached by phone."

Izzie followed me out of the SUV and started toward her building. She stopped and turned back. "I almost forgot to tell you. My friend Cal called to invite me to the first lady's visit to Martin Luther King Elementary School tomorrow. Do you want me to ask Cal if you can attend as well?"

"Cal? Is that the guy who works for the mayor? What do you know about him?" I had suspicions, but my question probably came off more like jealousy.

Izzie lifted an eyebrow. "We dated for a while, but now we're just good friends. He's been a great civil servant. I trust him. Does

172

that answer your question?"

I must have overstepped my current relationship. I just raised my hands in surrender before walking away, uneasy. Maybe it was because they dated. Maybe it was his continued friendship with Izzie. I couldn't sort it out in my mind, and with my upcoming evening meeting, or rather gunfight, with the Nightstalker, I didn't have time to think about it.

Once in my car, I called Zach to reschedule our meeting. If this could be my last action, then I needed someone to know who I was meeting and why.

Once at DeMarco's Pizza, I joined Zach in his regular booth.

He clapped me on the shoulder. "What's going on, big brother? I used every evasive move I learned from you and I can tell you that no one followed me."

I smiled. "Great work, thanks." No one followed him because Hesidence got the tails called off. Then again, Zach only needed to know that he did the right thing.

He shifted in his seat. "How did the meeting go with Hesidence?"

"Izzie's niece had some leads for us from her time in Afghanistan, but that isn't why I wanted to talk." I explained what I was doing.

He threw up his hands. "You better make another stop to see Mom. She would be upset if you didn't make one last visit. But what am I saying? One last visit! You'll come out of this victorious. You never lost any fight, ever! So, very simply, do you want to come over for dinner tomorrow night?"

"Not if you're cooking."

We both laughed, stood up, and hugged. I needed to keep Zach's words in my mind and in my heart. I also needed to heed his warning about seeing my mother.

CHAPTER 45

Richard Krauser, Director of the CIA, walked across the Presidential Seal woven into the carpet of the Oval Office and handed a copy of a letter to the director of Homeland Security, the director of the FBI, and the president.

After they finished reading it, Krauser jumped in. "Along with the letter, Agent Hesidence, on assignment in Pittsburgh, sent a video recorded by the suicide bomber on the phone of the American student who survived the attack. We've reviewed it. Although there are no details at this time, it is obvious that your wife will be in danger when she visits that school in Pittsburgh. How serious and to what degree we are not sure, but I agree with Hesidence's evaluation that it will most likely be something big."

The president leaned back and crossed his arms over his chest. "My wife's launch of her new program is of high priority." He frowned. "How reliable is the data?"

"We should have a full report in an hour or two." Krauser stifled the urge to tell the president everything they suspected. Until he had solid proof, the president wouldn't believe him.

Krauser was careful not to push the president in any direction. The President disliked the CIA, and therefore Krauser's job had been in jeopardy since the inauguration. Without analysis, Krauser had to hold back his gut feelings.

"Charles, what do you think?" The president directed his question to the DHS secretary.

"I can't say, Mr. President. Director Krauser has not shared all the information with me. I'll have to have my analysts go over it as well, then I may be able to give an opinion." He gave Krauser a sidelong glance with flared nostrils. "I do understand from my own sources that the video is several months old and was brought to light by a Pittsburgh police officer who is under suspension, suspected of murder." He shook his head. "It all sounds too contrived for me. I would say it is a desperate attempt by a desperate cop who's trying to save his own butt. I'll wait until I see everything before I pass judgment."

Krauser stiffened in his chair. His jaw tensed as he glared at Johnson. Johnson was leading the president down a dangerous trail. "I may be nothing but an old spook that has spent his life defending and protecting this country, but to me this seems like a credible threat worth investigating."

"You are an old spook from an ancient era, that's for sure," Johnson interrupted smoothly. "You see a terrorist behind every bush. Let my people examine the data. Personally, as I have stated before, I know we decimated the whole terrorist network. They don't have the reach to hurt us at home."

Krauser gritted his teeth and said nothing. What was the point of arguing in unfriendly territory?

Maggie Stern, the Director of the FBI, moved forward in her chair. "Mr. President, the Secret Service went over the school where your wife will make her presentation. Several times. I'll order a new search and tighten security," she said. "I guarantee her safety."

The president stood and clapped his hands. "Good. Now I've got to get to a meeting in Iowa. Keep me informed. Nadeem will remain here to collect the intelligence from the video and bring it to me, so funnel all information through her. Also, keep my advisory staff in the loop. It will most likely be an empty threat, but we can't take that chance."

The president moved toward the door.

* * *

In the hall, Nadeem waited for the president. The two walked out on the lawn toward the helicopter as he filled her in. "I need you to stay here and wait for the report from the CIA analysts, then bring it to me in Iowa immediately. I don't trust any of those three to give me what I need. Decipher their bull, and then join me after my dinner and speech."

She raised her voice over the whack-whack of the helicopter blades. "Mr. President, I know you feel Jack Hesidence is a solid agent, but I need to caution you that he's a reactionary and is not on board with your view of the broad terrorist problem. From what you said, this information came from a highly dubious source. I have a feeling this is all smoke and mirrors. Don't get drawn into it. I'll take care of it."

CHAPTER 46

Sabawoon Habibi emerged from his mountainside tent and answered his phone. "Yes."

The feminine voice on the other end of the line laid everything out for him. "There are complications you need to be aware of. The director of Homeland Security, the director of the FBI and the CIA chief just met with the president. They have some new information about our jihad efforts, but not enough to prevent our plans from going through. At least, not at this moment. I'm heading to the CIA facilities to intercept the information.

"After that, I join the president and will relieve his concerns." A delightful laugh flowed through the telephone. "I also heard the name of that soldier who killed your brother. He is involved. We have succeeded in making him the number one suspect. Dead or alive, he is a convenient scapegoat."

"How much do they know?" Habibi asked. "Are they keeping the president's wife from her public appearance? Do they have any names of my brothers in Pittsburgh? Is there any talk about a dirty bomb?"

"They have no idea about the bomb. They will beef up the security at the school but will not be able to defend against our attack." Nadeem paused. "Is your team taking care of all those who could tie this to us?"

"Most of them will be present at the school meeting. The only loose end is going to be that soldier. The assassin will take care of him," Sabawoon said.

Her voice crackled in the earpiece. "I don't think I have to remind you that if any of this gets out, I will be tried for treason. There is not much room for error."

The sternness in her voice rankled Habibi. A woman in his country would not talk to him so.

"The worst that can happen is that you will be martyred. Praise Allah!" Sabawoon said and hung up. It was time to set the next step in motion and eliminate this insolent female and loose end in the White House.

He dialed a number. When another Washington insider picked up the line, Habibi gave the command. "Strike her down. You know the timing." Then he disconnected the call. Satisfaction filled him like hot green tea.

CHAPTER 47

"You've come to say goodbye," Mom said as I plopped down in what I now considered my chair. She sat in her bed, the adjustable hospital bed raised behind her back, her walker ready at hand.

"I just got here. Why should I say goodbye already?" It was eerie that she already knew what was on my mind. "Why would you say that?"

"Solomon told me," she answered as she fiddled with the straw in a plastic cup. "He didn't say why, but he laughed heartily afterward. That man is just so full of life. I wish I had just a portion of his vitality." She let out a long sigh and made goo-goo eyes that made me blush.

"Why would he laugh?"

"He said he already gave you the secret. All you need to do is remember it at the right moment. Then there will be no need for goodbyes." She set down her cup and looked me in the eyes. "He thinks you lack faith. You always were the kind of kid who questioned everything. I guess you need a practical lesson in faith." She shook her head.

I stood and started pacing. "I had a lesson like that when Dad passed away. I believed God would heal him. I believed God would heal you. I believed God would work out everything with me and Izzie." I punctuated each statement with an emphatic jab of an index finger in the air, and my volume increased. "I had

179

faith, but God never delivered. How do you have faith in a God who keeps robbing you of the people you love?"

I had never said those things aloud before. I had thought them but never put them into words. Fortunately, she would forget what I said by the time I walked out the front door.

I finished a circuit of the small room and decided it was time to sit down.

"I am glad you finally admitted it," Mom said as she sat back. "The prodigal has finally admitted what drove him away. Don't you think it's time to come back home?" She was not only lucid, but sounded more like the mother I grew up respecting than she had in the last two years.

"Not yet, Mom. I have some serious business to attend to this evening that requires the best of the worst side in me. When that's done, then I'll consider 'coming back home,' as you say." Until then, I need the bad cop side of me to prevail."

"Solomon said his father David never went into battle without making sure he was walking hand in hand with the Lord. I think it's a lesson you need to learn. You've been doing life all by yourself—or at least you think you have, since your father died." The talking seemed to wear her out, and she lowered the head of her bed.

"Time for a nap?"

"No, time to pray for my little boy, Jude. Do what you have to do, and then tomorrow bring me some soup from Angela's."

"Angela's is closed," I reminded her.

"Go to her house. She's making me soup tonight. I am counting on you, so don't let your mother down. I want my soup for dinner tomorrow."

I made a mental note to tell Zach to pick up the soup. Just in case....

I left Mom deep in prayer, although it could have been a nap. I was not about to disturb her either way.

Outside, dusk had dissipated, leaving behind the blackness of night. No moon peeked through the wintry skies. I pulled up my collar up against the air, which had cooled while I visited Mom. But my senses were alive with the thought of what I needed to do.

A gunshot split the air. A bullet struck the wall next to my car, splintering the cement stones. I spun as I crouched, just in time to see a dark vehicle burn rubber on the road that passed in front of the Baptist home. The Nightstalker had sent me a calling card. It was time.

CHAPTER 48

My plan was to get to the meeting place ahead of him, but it appeared his plan was the same. He sped toward the church campus.

But I still had the advantage, because I knew the area. Instead of racing behind him, I headed behind the Baptist Home and urged my Chevelle up the hill. I should beat him by a few minutes. That would be all the time I needed to gain the higher ground. At least that was what Zach and I called it when we'd played behind the church.

A cold, hard rain started to fall. I parked my car at the church and pulled my long leather coat from the back seat before popping the trunk open. Snapping open the gun cases, I retrieved my Army Ranger sniper rifle and some ammo. I placed a spare handgun in the waistband of my pants, in case.

My mood was grim, my hands steady. The Nightstalker wouldn't go down easy, but this was my turf, and he had threatened my mother. I remembered Mom's advice. "God, be with me," I whispered. Not much of a prayer, but at least we were back on speaking terms.

"I am." The voice seemed to come from nowhere and everywhere at the same time.

I spun around, expecting to see the Nightstalker already upon me.

Nobody was there.

I wiped the chilling rain from my eyes and tried not to think about it any more as I jogged toward the crest of the small hill at the back of the church campus. When Zach and I played army here as children, this was the coveted spot. The one who made it first always won.

I held onto that thought as I leaped up the hill in the darkness and rolled myself flat behind a fallen tree. I had barely concealed myself when the sound of a car pulling into the parking lot reached my ears.

He was here.

The driving rain reduced visibility and prevented me from firing, so I watched. Several streetlights gave the parking lot a hazy glow.

A shadowy, dark form with a limp moved quickly toward my car. He pumped two bullets into a tire before heading in the direction of a large tree alongside the parking lot, keeping the car between us.

I swore under my breath. That was one more reason why the man had to go down. He injured my classic car.

The quick view of his profile showed that my foe wore night vision goggles. One strike against me. He also carried a scoped rifle. Two strikes against me.

Then heavy rain clouded what I could see. I had to wait. And if I fired too soon, I'd give away my position. I needed to be cautious and wise. I could use the wisdom of Solomon at this point.

The rain slacked off slightly, and the Nightstalker moved skillfully to the next tree, though he favored one foot. I had no clear shot.

"Detective Cameron." His voice cut through the sound of the pelting rain. "I had a pleasant visit with your mother today. It is sad what has happened to her mind, but I promise that she won't live long enough to remember the loss of her beloved son. She will be my last."

I refused to give in to his attempt to goad me into speaking in order to get a location. This wasn't my first rodeo. As I kept silent, however, anger and determination swelled inside me.

"Jude."

It was Dad's voice behind me. I twitched. The tension was playing on my unwrapping nerves.

"And to think this is a churchyard," Dad continued.

I couldn't afford to be distracted right now, so I ignored his voice.

He spoke again. "I remember when you and Zach used to play out here. You never knew that I stood at my window and watched the two of you. I knew then that you would enlist. You thrived on that sort of excitement." The voice I knew so well scared me and comforted me at the same time.

"Dad, you need to keep it down a little." My whisper was out of hearing range for the Nightstalker. At that point I realized, real or not, my father's presence was now entirely real to me.

"He can't hear me, Jude. Only you can hear me."

I whispered, "I am trying to wait for my best shot. He visited Mom earlier today and threatened her again just now. This fight has a lot more riding on it than just me against him."

"I know. That's why I decided to join the cause. Your mom was my everything. I loved her and still love her dearly. You must protect her, and I'm here to help. That Bozo threatened the wrong family."

The Nightstalker fired a shot about twenty feet to my right. Surely he couldn't have heard me whispering from such a distance. No, he was just trying to draw me out. I didn't flinch or budge, even when his next shot struck a tree three feet to my right. I glanced around me. Something had to be giving away my position. He was honing in on me too well.

His third shot whizzed past, barely to my left, kicking up

grass, mud and leaves.

"Detective!" shouted the Nightstalker, "I walked the campus early today. I know there is only one hiding spot. Field advantage may be yours, but the tactical advantage is mine. Your Army Ranger experience was too long ago. You've grown soft, sitting at a desk and eating donuts. Like all infidels, you lack the will to kill to protect your way of life. That is why our jihad will prevail. You are soft and arrogant."

His next shot hit the downed tree trunk I lay behind and spit mud and bark in my face. He knew my position, but he was the one who had grown arrogant.

Since he knew where I was, I spoke. "I've been reading the Bible lately. I came across this verse in the Book of Proverbs. It says, 'An evil man seeketh only rebellion: therefore a cruel messenger shall be sent against him.' The true God has sent me. Prepare to meet your cruel messenger." I rolled to my right. The fallen tree left a slight gap between the ground and the bottom of the trunk, a gap that I remembered. I was protected. But did I have a clear shot?

As the Nightstalker shifted slightly from behind his protective tree to fire, I pumped out a three-shot blast. The shells splintered the tree and showered him. I withdrew the rifle and rolled to the left to my earlier spot.

A barrage of gunfire tore apart my former position. The shots were wild, but the sheer number of them would have at least wounded me if I hadn't anticipated his response.

My next shot over the top of the log caused my enemy to cry out and rattle off a stream of obscenities in his native tongue. His return shots told me that wherever I hit him, it wasn't serious.

I was checking my ammo when footsteps splashed in the mud as he hurried to a tree a yard closer to me. I hadn't anticipated that move. His next few shots dug into the dirt near my head. He was too close.

"Looks like you got him right where you want him," Dad's voice joked from behind me.

I glanced back at his dark form. "I don't need comments from the peanut gallery, Dad." Frustration filled my tone, but the air broke open again as another shot thumped into the thick trunk of the tree.

Dad crawled up beside me, solid and yet not solid. He didn't miss a beat. "Remember the time the youth group had a paint ball battle back here? Your mother tore into me for allowing you kids to traipse through her flower beds. I was in the dog house for a week," he snickered.

"This is the real thing, Dad. Any splattering liquids will be my brains, not paint." Another shot hit the trunk on the other side of my head. "See what I mean?"

"You're missing the point. Your brother led the opposing army. They had you pinned down right here, and Zach was behind the same big tree Bozo is behind now. Do you remember what you did?"

"Yeah. I told them I was surrendering. When Zach stepped out to accept my surrender, I pelted him with a dozen paint balls. I don't think he has ever forgiven me for that." I chuckled.

"It worked once. Try it again," Dad said as he rose to hands and knees.

What a crazy idea. "This guy is no kid. It won't work this time."

"Just start the negotiations, then roll down the hill. I'll take care of the distraction." Dad was already crawling away from me.

"Listen, it's crazy enough that I'm talking to a figment of my imagination, but I don't see how something that exists only in my head, brought on by severe stress and a possible concussion, can distract a living, breathing killer." My voice was filled with frustration.

Dad stopped and looked at me over his shoulder. His image grew more solid and I saw his piercing dark eyes. It was the look he gave me as a child when he asked me to do a serious mission. "You've been called to be this man's cruel messenger. Just do as I told you, and you'll deliver a message from the true God to an evil force."

How could I argue?

I called out to my foe, "There's no way out. I'll step out from behind the hill if you promise one thing."

"I am a reasonable man. What do you want in exchange for your sacrifice?"

"Spare my mother." Then I began the slow, silent roll across the cold ground to the low end of the hill.

"I can do that. Stand up, without your weapons, and walk toward me," he said.

A ghostly figure rose from my former position. It crested the little hill and took two steps down the slope.

The Nightstalker stepped out from behind the tree that sheltered him. As I held fire, he sent several blasts through the apparition.

He took another step but stumbled on his bad foot.

Before he could notice that the bullets had no effect or that the apparition dissipated into the driving rain, I took aim, held my breath, and squeezed the trigger.

Two bullets entered his head. His body slumped against the tree and slid to the ground. I laid my rifle on the ground, stood and cautiously approached, gripping my handgun tightly.

The rain fell harder, as though to shroud the dead.

When I reached his body, I raised the Glock and fired two more rounds into his already exploded forehead. One was for the threat to my mother and the other was for my car. He had met his cruel messenger.

Headlights swerved into the parking lot. A car screeched to

a halt.

"Hands in the air and drop the weapon." Ed Rivers' voice cried out in sharp command.

"It's me, Ed. We have one less terrorist, but I have a feeling there are several more to go before it's over."

CHAPTER 49

Ed reported the Nightstalker's death. He decided not to mention my name in the report. We didn't have the time for me to sit in a holding cell while the justice system cleared my name.

I sneaked into my apartment through the back door to get dry clothes and try to sleep. I was sure that Jack Hesidence had gotten the heat off my back, but if there was one assassin, there could be more. It was one of the many possibilities that continually raced through my brain. Sleep was elusive, so I sat on the couch staring into the black, silent darkness.

The stress of all the recent events, along with the rap on my head in Cleveland, left me teetering on the edge between sanity and insanity. First, I heard my dead father's voice, then it had progressed to seeing him, then believing he interacted with the Nightstalker before I gunned him down. Either I was hallucinating, or something beyond me was pressing me to see and hear things I had not thought possible.

I raised myself from the chair and crossed the room in the total darkness to the bottle of scotch I kept in the kitchen. My mind continued racing in circles around the track that had become my life. At times I was sure I was as crazy as my mother, especially when I felt the need to meet her elusive boyfriend, King Solomon. Yet his clues, or leads, or whatever I chose to call them, had been right on the money every time. There was no coincidence in this. Whoever he was, he had solid intel, and I needed to know where

189

it came from.

I poured the scotch into a glass and carried it cautiously back to my chair. The first sip burned as it rolled across my tongue into my throat. I sat still, balancing my drink on the arm of the chair, as my thoughts did another lap around the track. The darkness in the room gave way to early dawn.

I needed to leave while I still had the cover of night to protect me.

Before I rose from the couch, my phone rang.

"Jude, the video analysis came back," Hesidence said. "We need to talk right away. Can you meet me in Tom's parking lot in five minutes?"

"I'll be there." I slipped out my apartment door and down the back staircase, into the basement, and out an alley window.

I parked the Chevelle behind Tom's and stepped into the waiting Suburban.

Hesidence's pale face scared me more than the encounter with the Nightstalker. He turned the laptop so I could see the screen and pushed the play button on the video. "This is some serious stuff. I don't know how the suicide bomber kid got it, but it confirms many of my suspicions. Unfortunately, it is still not a clean copy. The agency techs promised to have me a cleaner version this morning, but there was a snag."

CHAPTER 50

Nadeem had been in the CIA building many times before, on official and unofficial business. She had made friends in an inappropriate way with key gatekeepers, which allowed her access to items others would have no use for.

Tonight, she needed her close friend in the technology wing to give her access to the video from the jihadist's phone before it went back to the directors of the three agencies.

Nadeem stood in the doorway of CIA video technical department. Her presence anywhere in D.C. was tolerated because of her relationship with the president.

"Raj, are you working late again?" She leaned against the door frame to affectionately kid the CIA's number one video technician.

The technician startled at her voice, but quickly teased back. "Yes, I am, beautiful. Are you here to keep me company, or is it official business?" She loved the way his eyes drank her in. His distinct attraction fed her need for power.

"Sorry, but it's all business tonight. The president wants this info brought to him, like, an hour ago. Since your boss would rather sleep than do his duty, I volunteered to expedite it. I have a helo waiting for me at the White House." She ran her soft hand along his shoulder. Raj jerked beneath her fingers, as though a bolt of electricity ran through him.

"I promise to make it up to you next week. How about dinner

at my place?" Nadeem purred with well-trained seductiveness. "And make sure you bring a toothbrush."

"I would like that a lot." He pulled open a desk drawer. "Let me put a copy on a thumb drive for you to take it to the president."

"Excellent. Who else has it?"

"No one, really. I emailed a copy off to the agent who sent me the video, a guy named Hesidence. It was pretty rough, and not nearly as telling as my audio enhanced version. The clean version is terribly shocking. I'm glad the president is getting it right away. He needs to see this immediately."

"Where's the dirty version? POTUS may want to see that too." She leaned her chin on his shoulder, allowing him to inhale her perfume.

Raj pointed to the files on the screen. He copied both onto the thumb drive and handed it to her.

Nadeem put a hand behind his neck and pulled him to her. She gave him a deep kiss and nipped at his lip. With her free hand, she slipped the thin needle of a syringe into the side of his neck. The drug it pumped into him would put him to sleep in thirty seconds and cause a heart attack in thirty minutes.

As Raj slumped in his chair, she swung her arm around the man and held him in place as if he were still talking. Nadeem highlighted the files and deleted them, then plugged a flash drive into the computer and ran her program to write over the deleted files, making them impossible to recover. She smiled and left the room. Surveillance would simply show her following the President's orders.

When she landed at the Quad Cities Airport in Moline, Illinois, a limo whisked her to the Jumers Casino Hotel for the president's morning briefing. As she entered the room, the president stopped speaking and addressed her. "Yes, Nadeem?"

"It was a sad story of unrequited love, Mr. President. As was stated in your meeting with the Department directors, this cop in Pittsburgh is looking for a conspiracy in order to clear his name. There's nothing there. I will show it to you later today."

The president thanked her and returned to his other briefings.

Nadeem took her place in a chair along the wall. In a little while, she would need to contact Rafi to say that Hesidence was sent a poor-audio copy of the video, and that she alone had the enhanced-audio copy.

CHAPTER 51

Abdul nodded to Rafi and carefully closed the back door of the van so as not to jostle the nuclear device. The vehicle sat inside the garage they used as their meeting place.

"Do you have your weapon?" Rafi asked.

Abdul nodded.

"Are you prepared to use it?"

"I am a mujahideen." Rafi drew himself up to his full height and lifted his chin. "The Americans have killed our innocent children for hundreds of years. As the Holy Koran says, 'And We ordained for them therein a life for a life, an eye for an eye, a nose for nose, an ear for an ear, a tooth for a tooth, and for wounds as legal retribution.'"

Abdul smiled broadly. "Then let us meet Ebdullah and his bus of infidel children who would grow up to kill our children. Today is the Day of Reckoning. Allahu Akbar!" He hugged his friend.

* * *

Ebdullah pulled his school bus out of the parking lot and onto the main road. Ten minutes to first pickup.

The first child was a hyper-active but bright boy named Aaron. After he climbed up the steep steps, he selected a seat behind the driver. "Mr. Eb, this is going to be a great day at school," the boy announced as he bounced from one side of the seat to the other.

"I have heard, my friend. Today a very important person is speaking at your school," Eb answered, with a smile that each child had grown to trust. "Before I pick up the next student we have time to talk more about our faith in Allah. After all these months you should know quite a lot about Islam and the Prophet Mohammed. What would you like to ask me today?" This was the one child he felt had converted.

"Do you think there will be television cameras there? Do you think I will get on TV?" Aaron snapped out his questions quickly.

"I do hope they are there." Eb caught the boy's wide eyes in his large rearview mirror. It would be a historic day.

Looking at the freckled face in the reflection, a heavy feeling settled into Eb's stomach. This day would end young Aaron's life on earth. The lively questions and bright smile would be no more.

Eb forced himself to look away. Aaron would understand when he reached paradise that his sacrifice was for a holy war.

As the other kids boarded the bus, they sang songs, played games and ate candy as they did each morning. Their joy at the prospect of meeting the first lady spread from one child to another. Laughter broke out several times for no apparent reason.

All seemed normal until Ebdullah made a right turn down an old dirt road. "Where are we going?" asked Marylee, from the third row behind Ebdullah. Eb scowled then simply shook his head. He could have predicted that the overly friendly and effusively talkative girl would say something first.

"There is road construction ahead. I am taking a detour, but let's turn this into a wild amusement park ride. I'll go fast, and you hang on because the potholes are going to bump you up and out of your seat. It will be a blast." Ebdullah studied the children in the mirror. "Are you ready?"

His cheerful attitude quickly infected the children. They all screamed, "Yes!" including Lily, who usually complained about detours or anything different from the norm.

As the bus reached a fork in the road, Eb cut the steering wheel toward a graying, weathered barn with a sagging roof.

The kids fell silent and then began a chorus of questions. Lily stood in the back, her cell phone clutched in one hand. "Where are we going? This isn't the school, and this isn't a detour."

The fretful girl had probably sent her mommy a text. But it wouldn't matter. Even if her mom contacted the school or the police, by the time they decided to take her seriously — if ever — it would be too late.

Ebdullah answered the questions by jamming on the brakes.

The children slipped off of their cheap, plastic-covered seats and slammed hard into the metal backs of the seat ahead of them. Yells, cries, and tears erupted from their now-bruised faces as they raised their heads in time to see a second man board the bus carrying an AK-74-a, the 5.45 mm version of the AK 47.

The children's round eyes stared at the weapon pointed their direction.

"Sit in your seats and shut your mouths," yelled the side of Ebdullah he had never shown the children.

The commotion quieted, with the exception of numerous soft whimpers.

Ebdullah rose from his seat with rolls of duct tape hanging on his arms like bracelets.

The boy in the seat across the aisle from Aaron shook his head violently as Ebdullah approached him. Ebdullah ripped off a strip of the silvery tape and pressed it over his mouth. The boy kicked at Ebdullah, who knelt and wrapped his muscled arms around the boy's legs, then wrapped the tape around them several times. Finally, he grabbed the boy's hands and taped his palms together in the position for prayer.

He continued down the aisle, taping each child the same way. When one child stood with his arms crossed over his chest and refused to cooperate, Abdul shot off several rounds through the roof. "That is what will happen to the next child who does not do as he is told."

The boy almost melted back into his seat. He didn't move a muscle as Ebdullah taped his mouth, his ankles, and his hands, but Ebdullah recognized the hatred in the boy's eyes. It was a mirror image of the hatred that blazed in the eyes of children in his country toward the Americans.

He saved young Aaron for last. To him, he spoke. "Your final lesson in your new Islamic faith is that of Jihad. We are in a holy struggle against the infidels. They have killed innocent Muslims around the world. Today we strike back, and you will have the opportunity to become a holy warrior, a mujahideen, a jihadi. Today, this very day, you will be with Allah in paradise. And Aaron, not that it will make any difference to you right now, but Allah awaits you with seventy-two virgins."

Aaron seemed too scared to care, and his lips trembled.

Once the children were secured, the two men carried the nuclear device onto the bus, placing it carefully between the bolts that Eb had installed months before. They secured the device on a cushioned base. Although it was reasonably safe in its non-activated state, they had to be careful as the bus maneuvered back along the rutted dirt road.

Ebdullah piloted the bus back the way they had come, Abdul standing beside him. They should arrive roughly fifteen minutes behind the last bus.

By the time he pulled up to the school entrance, it would be too late to stop the Day of Reckoning. His detonator was already taped to his hand. Even a kill shot would trigger it once Abdul armed the bomb. If they were able to kill him before he could press the button, there were two other detonators. One would be with Khaliq and other would be on Hamid.

No one could kill all three before one of them detonated the bomb—annihilating the school, the city, and of course, the first lady of the United States.

CHAPTER 52

"What do we have, Hesidence?" I sat huddled with him in the back of his Suburban, looking at the fuzzy end of the video that had just flashed by.

"The tech in Washington said he would send me a cleaner audio copy later, but thought I might get some intel off of this copy for now. We take what we can get. It confirms what Mahmood wrote in his letter. The dead kids were used to ship heroin back to this country. Amin is tied into it. What I wanted you to see is this still frame." He opened a photo file.

I sucked in a deep breath as Hesidence zoomed in on an image of a snapshot pinned to a wooden plank by a wide knife blade. It was a copy of the picture on my military ID when I served in Afghanistan.

"I like his attention to detail." Hesidence chuckled. "He put the knife right in your neck."

I shook my head with disgust.

Suddenly all business, Hesidence said, "I haven't put the whole plan together yet, but I am fairly sure Habibi chose Pittsburgh and has had a hand in pulling you into this.

"Miller knew too much, plus Habibi knew his death would get you emotionally involved." Hesidence tapped a finger on the keyboard. "The deaths of the teens in Afghanistan might have been to smuggle drugs into the U.S., but I sense there's more to it."

I shook my head. Puzzling.

Hesidence snapped the laptop closed. "Right now, I need to get to the school for the first lady's detail. Since you and Rivers aren't assigned to it, hang near the periphery. If you see or hear anything, contact me."

The Suburban pulled away from the parking lot behind Tom's the moment I stepped out, but I hadn't even reached my car before Ed called.

"Jude, the acting captain still wants you to turn yourself in. I told him I'd talk to you about it. Okay, so I talked to you about it. Now, where do you want to meet?"

"I just saw the video from Gloria's phone. Most of it was unintelligible, but it was obvious that I've been the target of that Taliban leader whose brother I killed. He vowed to kill me back then, and I don't think he is done trying."

"Bad news," said Ed.

"Right now, Hesidence wants us to help with the first lady's event at the elementary school. I'm behind Tom's Diner. Meet me here."

I waited next to my car.

Ed arrived in less than ten minutes. I heard him before he pulled into the parking lot in his old hunting and fishing truck. The thing rattled into a spot and wheezed when Ed turned off the ignition. Ed loved the rough, redneck mystique and drove it sometimes when he wanted to travel more like a local and less like a cop.

I climbed in, and he gave the dashboard a few pats. "Good old Liberty Belle. Now tell me what Hesidence wants us to do?"

"Keep our eyes and ears open," I told him.

CHAPTER 53

Against the wall of the crowded school cafeteria, Hesidence shifted in his wheelchair and with an act of will kept himself from fidgeting with the wire buried in his collar. He wore blue jeans and a Steelers sweatshirt today, part of his often-used disguise. A paraplegic is usually overlooked as a threat.

His stomach was uneasy. Something big was up. But what was it?

Dignitaries and Secret Service agents mingled among the students and teachers in the Martin Luther King Elementary School cafeteria. In the corners, television reporters stood in front of cameras, speaking into microphones to their viewers at home. Students, teachers, Secret Service agents, reporters and camera people crammed the rest of the room.

Standing near Hesidence and speaking into a cell phone, the principal seemed to be keeping tabs on a late arriving bus. They'd miss the opening.

The wire concealed in Hesidence's ear crackled to life as the tech in the Suburban spoke. "Hesidence. We picked up from the encrypted frequency on the police scanner a report that a child texted her mother from her school bus, something about being kidnapped. A second child also texted something unintelligible to his parents. It was about twenty minutes ago."

Hesidence took a deep breath. "Details, please."

"They mentioned the phone numbers, and I've picked up

and mapped the signal from the cell phones. It's taking the local police much longer to do the same thing. I can see that the phones are in the same vehicle, apparently headed toward the school where you are."

Hesidence shook his head. "Tell Cameron to follow up. Keep me up to date."

The high level of sound in the cafeteria came down a notch when Mayor Budding approached the microphone. He smiled his politician smile and cleared his throat. "Today, our city and this school have a very special guest. She needs no introduction, I am sure. Let me tell you what a great lady she is, and then ask you to give her a big round of applause."

Cal, the mayor's assistant, reached out his hand to help the first lady rise from her chair. He walked with her to the podium. As she turned to thank the mayor and Cal for their assistance in the project, she looked down, and shock crossed her face.

Hesidence raised his head and twisted in order to see. A gun. The man held a gun to her ribcage. How had it gotten through the tight security?

A second terrorist pulled his weapon from a hiding spot in a cleaning cart and waved it over the crowd.

"Please keep your cameras running," Cal said. "I want the world to know that we, in the oppressed Muslim world, are willing to sacrifice ourselves for Jihad, our holy war. I ask that the security details place their weapons on the cafeteria tray that my fellow mujahideen is rolling past them."

One Secret Service agent made a move. He was shot in the head for his effort. Children screamed as his body thudded to the floor.

Cal continued, "Because of that stupid move, everyone but the camera people must lie down on the floor. On your stomachs." He stopped and looked at the stunned faces staring at him. "Did nobody hear me? I said down on the floor!"

Amid the rustling of people obeying his command, Cal continued, "As I speak, a school bus filled with children is heading toward us. It carries a nuclear bomb. I have two fellow mujahideen in the bus. Each of us wears a trigger device that will detonate the nuclear weapon. If you shoot me, then one of the others will render this part of the state a radioactive wasteland."

A low groan came from the crowd.

Cal went on. "If the bus is delayed by the police, then my fellow mujahideen will kill one child for every minute of delay."

Hesidence, still seated, murmured into his wire, "Has Cameron located the bus?"

* * *

Ed, driving the ancient pickup truck, looked at me.

I spat out, "Finding that bus will be impossible."

"Not especially, partner. All buses approach the school on a one-way route. If we take Jones Street up ahead we will hit Second Ave. That is the one-way street approach."

"And you know this how?" I lifted an eyebrow.

"My kids went there. I have a family, you know? All grown but I still remember the school route quite well." Ed's smile told me he was on top of things. "There! That has to be the bus."

The impossible just became possible.

Ed drew close to the bus' rear bumper. A boy in the back stared out the window at us with wide eyes. Duct tape covered his mouth.

CHAPTER 54

We bounced along the potholed street that the terrorists had chosen, hugging the bus' rear bumper. The two-way radio in my cell phone crackled to life.

"Cameron, this is Hesidence. We have a dire situation at the school. I hear you have eyes on the missing bus."

"Ed and I are following it now. The bus is full of kids, and a gunman is standing near the back with an AK. That's all I can see."

Hesidence's voice broke up, then cleared. "The lead terrorist here says they have a nuclear device inside the bus. If he's right, this city will be wiped out. But if anyone delays the bus, the children on board will be shot. This Cal guy, from the mayor's office, says they have multiple detonators. If one of the terrorists is shot, then one of the others will set it off immediately."

"How many detonators?" I asked.

"Maybe four. Two here and two on the bus. But I'm guessing."

As soon as Hesidence said "four," I remembered Solomon's tip. There are three. So far, the wise King had given valuable intel. I had to run with what I knew, and my gut told me this was true. "Hesidence, there are three of them. Trust me on this. My guess is that the bus driver has one. Ed is pulling us up next to him so I can get a better look."

My heart sank at what I saw. The man had a device taped to his hand. I could shoot him in the head, but that would cause his body to twitch, and that would set off the activated bomb. I passed that information on to Hesidence.

Hesidence, no doubt trying to be inconspicuous in the crowded cafeteria, let out a simple sigh of frustration. "How long before the bus arrives?"

I looked over at the bouncing bus, moving at no great speed. "About ten minutes."

Hesidence's voice dropped. "You'll have to make a precision shot that severs the brain stem. You will have one shot, but don't take it until you hear me shoot."

I shook my head. I'd heard about that too, in Afghanistan, where these detonators came from. "I'll be ready."

* * *

Hesidence switched his whispered conversation to his operative in the van outside the school. "You heard that, right? Detective Cameron will take out the terrorists."

"That is a tough shot," his fellow agent replied. "Don't you want me to get our snipers set to take it?"

"You didn't read Cameron's file, did you?"

"No, sir."

"Cameron was one of the top shooters in the Rangers. Just tell the snipers to let Jude pass; he's up to the job."

Hesidence's focus returned to the cafeteria, which now reeked of fear.

Cal spoke again. "My name is Khaliq, and today we strike a blow against the Great Satan. This city has one opportunity to prevent the justifiable deaths of all these children and the infidels of the community. Mayor, come here and secure the first lady's arms."

The mayor stood. "I will not be a part of this. I am an American. I am a patriot." He threw his arms over his chest.

Cal smirked and waved a handgun before him. The mayor's face fell.

What was that all about? Hesidence's nostrils flared. Something stank.

The mayor stepped behind the first lady and gripped her by the upper arms.

Hesidence could see that she struggled, but the tip of a large knife pressed into her back. It was held by the other terrorist, a man in a janitor uniform holding a large ceremonial knife in one hand and a rifle in the other. She glanced back and stopped struggling.

"Reporters!" Cal shouted. "Move those cameras closer." He kept his eyes on them as the cameramen stepped over people and repositioned themselves. When they slowed after closing in about ten feet, Cal waved for them to come closer. Finally, he held up a hand when they were only five feet away.

Cal took up his monologue again. "Today, my people, after centuries of oppression, will cut off the head of the Great Satan. We demand that all Muslim prisoners held in every jail, at Guantanamo Bay and at every military installation, be released immediately. If not," he waved an arm toward the first lady, still held by the mayor, "then I will behead your first lady in front of the world. We will strike a blow for the freedom of the Muslim people and as a symbol of the dawn of the new Caliphate."

Two Secret Service agents stood and took a step forward.

The second terrorist raised the tip of the blade to the first lady's throat. She kept her head high and faced forward, nostrils flared.

The terrorist pressed until a small rivulet of blood trickled down her neck onto her dress.

The agents stepped back.

The crowded room remained silent, except for the muffled whine of a child.

Cal smiled. To Hesidence, he looked like a guy confident of stepping shortly into paradise.

CHAPTER 55

I sat in the front of the truck as it neared the school, tension building in my hands and neck. I cracked my knuckles and frowned. How were we going to knock out all of these guys? In what order?

Hesidence had studied the two terrorists at the school. The second didn't have a detonator in hand, which meant Hesidence could put a bullet in Cal's head and then have a bit of time before going for the second one. I needed to coordinate my bullet for the bus driver with Hesidence's shot for Cal. And then I needed to shoot the second terrorist in the bus. Immediately.

I turned to Ed. "You heard. We have about five minutes before he beheads the first lady. That means Hesidence will take his shots in that time. I need to take my shots when he does." I relayed my plan.

"That Glock of yours won't do it, but Esmeralda would love to go to the dance with you." Ed grinned.

Yes, his hunting rifle had a name, too. I pulled her out from behind the seat and popped the caps off the top-of-the-line scope.

I was taking the risk and the shot. Not just because my country needed me to do it, but because through the whole ordeal of my recent life, I realized that the most important things in my life had been lost in the last few years. I wanted them all back, and one of the things I wanted most was inside the school with two terrorists. Once Izzie was safe, I would rebuild our relationship and marry her. But none of that would happen if I missed this shot.

* * *

The president and his staff sat in the penthouse suite in an Iowa hotel. His hands shook. "How did our intelligence people fail so badly? The world is about to watch the beheading of my wife on national TV, and all they can tell me is that they are working on it." He jumped to his feet and started pacing. "Nadeem, what do we know?" His voice cracked.

"The CIA director just came back on the phone line. I'm putting you on."

The president steadied his hand as he took the phone from her. "Rick, what do we know?"

"I am sure you are watching television. That is what is happening on the inside. The bus is pulling up to the school now. My snipers tell me that there is a device anchored to the bus floor. It is most likely nuclear. There is one gunman holding the children hostage and one driver," Krauser reported.

"Do we have a clear shot at them?" the president asked.

"We don't. Our snipers are not in the right places to hit either terrorist in the bus. Unfortunately, we did not anticipate this type of attack. We have learned that a shot to the driver would cause even a body twitch to set off the type of detonator being used. There are at least three detonators connected to the hands of different terrorists. A sniper would have to sever the brain stem or cut off the hand. Instantly."

"How do we know all that?"

"Agent Hesidence is inside, disguised as a paraplegic, and is not suspected. He is communicating with our people on the street. He also says he has an asset on the street that can take out the driver without causing a detonation," Krauser said.

"Who is the asset?" the president asked.

"A Pittsburgh police detective and former Ranger sniper. He

was one of the best they ever had, Jude Cameron."

Nadeem asked for a moment to brief the president.

"Rick, I need to put you on hold," the president said as he pushed a button on the phone. "What is it, Nadeem?"

"That is the rogue cop who shot his own captain. Hesidence is anything but a reliable agent. He is probably as close to rogue as can be. He runs his operations the way he wants. I don't think you should trust this line of intel or these two—as they say— cowboys. There has to be a way to negotiate out of this."

"What do you suggest, Nadeem?"

"We have Mayor Budding's cell number. Let's call it and talk to this Cal person. Give him what he wants."

"Put Krauser back on the line." The president drew in a breath. "Rick, we have a rogue cop killer in Cameron and half rogue agent in Hesidence. I am not putting my trust in them. Tell them both to stand down. I am taking another approach. I will negotiate with the terrorists."

Nadeem hung up the line and dialed Mayor Budding's phone.

The president found himself talking to Cal.

Cal's voice sounded stern. "Mr. President, what is your answer? Before you give in to my demands, I want to place you on speaker phone so all the world can hear." The president heard a click. "Please continue, Mr. President."

* * *

Hesidence narrowed his eyes. Cal was waxing long-winded about the further sins and weaknesses of America, with his and his partner's attention solidly trained on the cameras. It was time.

"Jude," he whispered into the wire. "My target is distracted. Are you ready to take your shot? We do it on my five count."

"Born ready, Hesidence."

"One, two, three, four...." A single shot echoed off the cafeteria walls.

The bullet passed straight through the upper lip of the terrorist and into the brain stem, blood spraying the first lady, the mayor, and the other terrorist as Cal dropped motionless to the cafeteria floor.

A half second later, Hesidence leveled his gun and took a second shot. It, too, passed through the upper lip of the second terrorist. The gunman never had the opportunity to pull his detonator from his pocket, if he had one.

After some seconds, Jude's voice spoke in his earpiece. "Therefore a cruel messenger shall be sent against him."

CHAPTER 56

We waited for word from Hesidence. Any second now.

It was time.

A cruel messenger. That was the role I had to play in this scene. "Lord, to protect these children and this nation, I pray for a steady hand and steady feet."

A calm came over me, and a quote from Mark Twain came back to my mind. I hadn't read it for years. "The two most important days in your life are the day you are born and the day you find out why." On this day I would find out why.

The bus crawled forward in front of the school, and Ed drove his truck slowly alongside the bus. I pushed open Liberty Belle's rusty door and swung back to the bed of the truck.

The gunman in the bus had his back turned to me as he stared down the police at the front of the school. He held his weapon's barrel to the temple of a hysterical child.

Two shots crackled through the cell-phone radio in my shirt pocket. Hesidence had done his job. I had half a second to do my part.

I steadied myself like a surfer riding the big wave. I raised Esmeralda and sighted the back of the driver's head just as the pickup truck banged deep into one of Pittsburgh's famous potholes. The thudding wheels sent a rolling shock-wave through Liberty Belle.

As a boy, I utilized the hills of Pittsburgh for a favorite sport:

skateboarding. My body, without thought, righted itself. I pulled myself back into position, but I had lost the optimum shot and the optimum timing. I drew in another breath to calm myself. I'd take the shot when God made the opportunity plain.

The bus driver applied his brakes and moved the gearshift into park. He looked into the sky, I suppose to praise Allah, when the bright morning sun broke through the clouds in a brilliant yellow beam of blinding light that struck the windshield of the bus. He moved his taped hand with the detonator up to shield his eyes, turned away from the sun, and saw me.

God had spoken. It was my moment. "A cruel messenger shall be sent against them." As I spoke the words, I lined up my sight and pulled the trigger. The window shattered, sending glass into his eyes. The bullet ripped through his upper lip, cutting through his brain stem and exiting out the rear of his head in a blossom of blood and brain matter before lodging in the roof of the bus.

I had no more than whispered a prayer of thanks to the Lord when Belle lurched to the side as Ed swerved to avoid a parked bus, sending me to my knees.

A sharp report of another rifle meant someone else, probably one of the rooftop snipers, had taken out the last jihadi.

Ed stopped the truck several yards down the road. I catapulted out of the back, ran to the driver's window, and wrapped an arm around his neck.

We watched as a crowd of panicked adults poured out of the school and converged on the school bus. Thank God they hadn't had to see their children die. That was what the Black Rose had been talking about.

The first lady left the building, surrounded by a mass of black suits. Her entourage sped away.

Hesidence strode out and found us quickly. We stood there staring at each other, words failing.

Two arms encircled my waist from behind. I remembered

those arms. They always felt good around me. I turned to see Izzie's beautiful face.

"Too busy saving the world to kiss a girl?" she said with a smile.

"Never." I pulled her closer and gave her a kiss she would never forget.

"What's next?" Ed asked.

Before I could answer, Hesidence jumped in. "We need to debrief all of you. I'll make it as quick as possible. I'll have agents drop by and take longer statements tomorrow. Both of you cops know the drill."

I nodded and took Izzie's arm. "Once we debrief, I have to go get some soup and deliver it to my mother. I forgot to ask Zach to do it. You know her. Mom will not be denied."

"Hey, Jude, what do you mean, soup?" Izzie asked.

I loved to hear her say my name. "This may sound a little crazy, but I need to grab some soup from an old friend of my mother's and take it to her before dinner tonight. She made me promise to do it, and you know how Edna is if you break your promise." I smiled.

"Need a co-pilot?" she asked with a grin. It was the grin I had missed and dreamed about for the last couple years.

"No, I actually need a ride. My car is back at Tom's. Is your car here?" I asked.

"Right over there." She pointed at a nearby parking lot filled with cars. "Where do we get the soup?"

"Remember Angela's Restaurant? Mom said Angela was making her soup last night and I was to pick it up. The restaurant is closed, but I remember where she lives." I extended my arm, and Izzie took it.

Each of us gave our statements. The EMTs patched my cuts, scrapes and bruises, and Ed gave a rousing description of our exploits that I barely recognized. Once the aftermath was cleared, so were we. Hours later, Izzie and I took her car to Angela's house.

When I knocked on the door, Angela looked shocked. "I can't believe this," she said. "I was making your mother's favorite soup last night and I kept thinking about her. Now, here you show up at my door. What can I do for you, Jude?" Angela gave me a big hug then looked at Izzie. "Oh my, is this little, skinny Izzie, all growed up?"

Izzie grinned back and said softly, "Hello."

I cleared my throat. "My mother said to come see you because you were making her soup. I assumed she had a nurse look up your number and call you," I said to the rotund woman, whose smile was as sweet as her pies.

"Nope. I got no call from her or a nurse, but I do have the soup. Then again, Edna was always a little clair—ah, what is that word?" she questioned with a finger, scratching at the air like the word was behind a cloud only she could see.

"Clairvoyant," Izzie answered.

"Yes, something like that. She would say things and I would say, 'how do you know that, Edna?' and she would say, 'God told me.'" Angela motioned for us to follow her to the kitchen. "I didn't know why I was packing up a quart, but here it is."

Izzie shook her head. "I guess God talks to you, too."

"You sound just like your Dad. I do miss that man. He was one of the good ones in this world. He was taken way too early. Now, you two take that soup and run along." She handed us the container and stood smiling. As we turned to leave, she said, "And don't forget to invite me to the wedding."

I tried to protest, but Izzie smacked me on the arm and whispered, "Remember, God talks to her." I grinned and agreed. Maybe my hope and my prayers were beginning to be answered yes.

When we arrived at the Baptist Home, it was a few minutes before five. I had made it on time for dinner, as promised.

My mother was already pulling on her slippers, the ones that the fictitious George had sent from Germany. "Soup's here!" I announced loudly.

"What took you so long?" Edna grumbled. "I assumed that you had forgotten, like usual. So I made arrangements to attend the school dinner. Maybe you could be a good son, for once, and get my wheelchair. My legs are hurting today. You can push me down to the restaurant." She stopped talking and took a good, long look at us both. "What happened to you two? You look like you were in a fight."

"It's a long story, Mom. I will come by tomorrow morning and give you all the details." I glanced over at Izzie.

"You two also look like you need a vacation. I suggest Mexico. It is a great place for a honeymoon," she quipped, with a sly grin on her face.

"Mom!" I said in mock surprise.

Izzie backhanded my arm once again and whispered, "Hey, God talks to her, too."

I shook my head and put the soup into the tiny fridge, then helped my mother into her chair. We rolled out the door but got stuck in the wheelchair-and-walker traffic heading to the cafeteria. I looked up at the doors around me. I had never really taken the time to see the folks that surrounded Mom's room. After reading the nameplates: O'Donnel, Shelley; Keefer, David; Cipriani, Tony, my eyes fell on her next-door neighbor's. King, Solomon. Oh my, there really was a King Solomon!

"Izzie, look at that. It is King Solomon's room. I never thought that King Solomon could be a guy named Solomon King. It wasn't her imagination. He is real!"

"Oh, yeah, Solomon King. He was quite the civic leader only a decade ago. I enjoyed hearing him speak and loved it when Dad brought him around to the house. I wonder how he is doing?" Izzie touched the closed door.

215

A nurse standing nearby interrupted us. "Mr. King had a heart attack and is in a coma."

"Did it happen this morning?" I asked.

"No, less than a week ago. He had just come in and then the heart attack," the nurse said. "No one ever got a chance to even speak to him. We don't expect him to last out the day. Poor man. Your mother sat with him most days just talking away. I was glad he had somebody."

I turned to Izzie. "That was when Mom started in on the King Solomon stuff." Izzie stroked my back. I think she was encouraging me not to solve that mystery and just accept what had happened. I leaned down next to my mother's ear and said, "I'm home, Mom."

She patted my hand and said, "Good. I hope they killed the fatted calf, because I am starving."

EPILOGUE

Nadeem stood next to the desk of the Oval Office and breathed deeply. The meeting had gone fairly well, considering.

The Directors of the CIA, the FBI and the Homeland Security Secretary had just been dismissed from the Oval Office, along with some other cabinet members. The president, still seated on the couch where he sat for the meeting, trembled with anger, anger he'd expressed at the three in the form of a tongue-lashing.

Clearly, he was extremely upset. Nadeem composed her features into a sympathetic, concerned look.

He looked up at her and shook his head, frowning. "What do I do now, Nadeem? They all failed, but I can't replace all three at once. One has to go. The newspapers say it. The people say it. The cable news shows say it. I say it. No, I demand it. Eventually they all will be gone. But one of them has to be the scapegoat."

Smoothly, she gave her analysis. "Sir, the CIA completely failed in getting good intel prior to the event, but it was their man who saved the first lady. The FBI seemed clueless, but not at fault. And firing a woman would send a bad message that women cannot handle a job at this level. We don't want another war-on-women narrative." She cleared her throat. "That leaves Charles Johnson at DHS. Also, this was an attack on our Homeland. I believe the nation will be most happy if we hang him for the failure."

The president paused and nodded. "I agree with your

assessment. We will announce Johnson's departure from the Administration tomorrow. Keep it under your hat." The president rose from the couch and moved to his desk. "I don't want a resignation. I want the nation to see me fire him."

His shoulders rounded as the weight of recent events pressed down on him. "I need to get back to the nation's business. And by the way, I am naming you as the new head of Homeland Security. I trust you. Set up the press conference for prime time tomorrow night."

Nadeem smiled and left the room. She moved quickly to her office, retrieved her secure SAT phone and called Habibi.

"What does the president know?" Sabawoon asked.

"We were able to cover most of our loose ends here. Amin is still to be dealt with. I don't think he will last much longer — I have contacts inside the prison that will eliminate Amin and Budding. But to be honest, Amin knows only about the smuggling operation. He can talk all he wants." She bit her lip. "Unfortunately, the Pittsburgh locals that were helping Khaliq rough up friends of Jude Cameron have been arrested. The public's out for their blood. Also, several accomplices of Jude Cameron who had been arrested due to our work have been freed."

Habibi grunted. "Tell me some good news."

She cleared her throat. "I do have some good news. The president is firing Homeland Secretary Johnson tomorrow evening and appointing me to his position. I do believe that will give us more latitude for a larger and better coordinated attack." She couldn't keep a bit of glee out of her voice.

"Good, that is very good. Now, what about Jude Cameron? Is he in prison yet?" Habibi asked.

"No. He is an American hero. We will need to take a different route to settle your differences. I have an idea for that. As part of my new position, I will schedule a trip to Afghanistan. We will meet and talk face to face to set the next phase in place. Allahu

218

Akbar."

Perhaps Habibi could perform the execution of Jude Cameron himself. She disconnected the SAT phone and placed it back in her secured hiding place.

Dear Reader,

If you enjoyed this novel, please immediately click over to Amazon and/or Goodreads and leave a review. That will help spread the word and will be very helpful to me.

I've written other books as well, and there will be at least one sequel to this one. To find out more, look for my website at http://timothywayers.wix.com/author

—Timothy W. Ayers

ACKNOWLEDGMENTS

My three grandsons Jude, Cameron and Zach because I used their names (one of them said I stole his name), and they have been an integral part of my life.

My granddaughter Lily because I will steal her name in a future book.

My daughter Becca, who reads my books and likes them.

My brothers: Jack, who fact-checks all the cop stuff. Matt, who is the basis for the character of Zach. Ed because he is the basis for Ed Rivers. And Chris, because he is the basis for George from Germany, whom no one sees.

My friends at Boscov's who encouraged me and pushed me to get it done.

My friend Jody because she is the best critic I have and a wonderful friend and writer.

And the staff at Castle Gate Press because you made me a better writer, and that is a priceless gift.

ABOUT THE AUTHOR

Timothy W. Ayers is the author of *The Sign of the End* and several best-selling children's books. He received an Award for the Best Speculative Fiction for 2017 for his book, *Cruel Messenger*. Tim lives along the Mississippi River in an attempt to channel his inner-Mark Twain. When Tim is not turning out historical fiction alongside his co-author and grandson, Jude B. Rennie, he is plotting his next action thrillers.

www.ingramcontent.com/pod-product-compliance
Lightning Source LLC
Chambersburg PA
CBHW022016170626
46808CB00001B/445